Books
by Ashley Gardner

Captain Lacey
Regency Mysteries

Other Mysteries

Murder Most Historical

Ashley Gardner

A Collection
of Short Mysteries

Table of Contents

The

Bishop's

Lady

The Bishop's Lady

An Émilie d'Armand mystery

Paris, 1679

The Poullard hôtel did much to dispel my misgivings about returning to Paris. I had not been to the city often since my husband's death — the memories of creditors and the police assaulted me at every turn. But when my friend Aimee's carriage bore me through a gateway into the majestic courtyard of her father's home, and I spied the line of footmen waiting to assist me down, I realized how very different this visit to Paris would be.

Red-haired Aimee Poullard, with whom I shared a cramped bed at Versailles where we were ladies-in-waiting to the queen of France, met me in the elegant chamber that was to be my own for a fortnight. The chamber held a bed large enough for four, a gilded cupboard for my meager wardrobe, and not one, but three real chairs with cushions. At court, I was allowed to sit on nothing but stools, and then only when a senior lady was not present. I imagined I'd spend much of my visit hopping from chair to chair to chair, reveling in my luxury.

Aimee and I embraced as though we hadn't seen each other for months instead of only a few days. She'd gained a leave of absence to return home for a visit to her family, and remarkably, had obtained permission for me to stay with her. Aimee, for all her flightiness, was a favorite of the queen and had learned how to pry any favor she wanted out of Marie-Therese. It also did not hurt that her father was rich, not to mention loudly loyal to Louis of France.

Aimee released me and reclined in one of the damask-upholstered chairs to watch my maid Beatrice help me unpack.

"This was Angél's room," Aimee said, waving a languid hand at the portrait over the fireplace.

A young woman with doe-like eyes gazed down at us from a painting that had been competently though not brilliantly done. She had light brown curls arranged in a style of five years ago, which trickled over a bodice that was cream-colored and virginal.

"She was married to my brother, Renaud," Aimee went on. "One evening, we found her dead at the bottom of the staircase."

I thought of the steep and creaking staircase I'd traversed to reach this room and suppressed a shiver. A tumble from it would doubtless kill anyone. I had a sudden and unnerving vision of the lovely young woman lying broken on the slates three floors below, her hair splaying over her lifeless face.

The morbid image dissolved as Aimee came off the chair to crush me in another perfume-and-satin scented hug. "I am so glad you've come, Émilie. I will show you the Paris your husband never let you see. I promise you myriad delights." She kissed my cheek, flashed me a dimpled smile, then left me alone.

Beatrice, who shared my vivid imagination, gazed up at Angél's portrait in worry. When she caught my eye, she gulped, crossed herself, and began to frantically stuff my gowns into the cupboard.

Beatrice was not a good maid, but she was steadfast and loyal, and best of all, cheap. My husband, Marcel D'Armand, had left me with next to nothing, and at the moment, I lived upon the charity of Madame de Montespan, the Sun King's former mistress. Though I nominally worked for the queen, it was Montespan I needed to keep happy. She was not pleased that I'd wanted to leave for two weeks, but she had grudgingly conceded to let me go. The queen had given permission, and Montespan wouldn't risk annoying the king by defying her.

Montespan let others believe she liked having me about because of my shrewd observations of members of the court, but the truth was that I knew things she was keen to keep secret. I was not proud of my hold over her, but when one's husband dies in scandalous circumstances, leaving his wife destitute and facing life on the streets or in prison, one does whatever one must to survive. Marcel had been a reckless gambler, but whenever he'd won, he'd taken not only money but knowledge as payment. Thus, though he'd not left me a sou, I'd found some very interesting notes among his meager belongings.

Beatrice dressed me for supper in a pale silk gown whose bodice bared my neck and top of my bosom, and placed each of my dark curls across my shoulders with care. When a servant came to fetch me, I followed him to the perilous staircase. The footman, adolescent and agile, skimmed his way down and disappeared into the hall, while I gripped the banister and shuffled along in my high-heeled slippers.

I wondered if Angél had been hurrying down to supper, as I was now, when she'd slipped on the polished wood and lost her footing in her awkward shoes. I stopped, clutched the rail, and squeezed my eyes shut.

When I opened them again, a man in red velvets was striding into the empty passage below. Candlelight flared on a gold crucifix studded with gems that hung against his chest, and on fiery hair that was the same color as Aimee's. He moved like a young man, and when he turned to look upward, I saw that his handsome face was unlined, his eyes sharp and glittering.

He caught sight of me and halted, his lips parting in shock. He stood fixed in place for a long moment, then he said, very softly, "Angél?"

I didn't move, uncertain I'd heard correctly. The man studied me for a few moments of silence, then, with the impatience of one who disliked waiting for anything, put his foot on the bottom stair and started for me.

I quickly descended a few steps until I was in the candlelight. "No. It is Madame D'Armand, Aimee's friend."

The man stopped. Color flooded his face, his eyes flashing with rage, then I saw him carefully mask all emotion, leaving his expression as blank as parchment.

"I beg your pardon, Madame," he said, his voice abruptly neutral. "Shall we go in to supper?"

He waited for me to reach him, then he

escorted me through the echoing house, his face shuttered, his blue eyes cool.

The Poullard family had already gathered in the supper room by the time I and my velvet-clad escort reached it. Monsieur Pollard, a square-faced, solemn man in a long black wig, took his place at the head of the table. Aimee's brother, Renaud, a staid young man with red hair—the one who'd been married to Angél—sat on his right. Renaud's second wife, Mathilde, looked steady enough—rotund and sensible—the sort of woman who would never tumble carelessly down the stairs to her death.

Aimee's oldest brother, Michel, looked much like the younger, and he too had married a solid, sensible wife called Léonore. Madame Poullard, Aimee's mother, rounded out the slow placidity of the family.

The only color at the table came from the vivacious Aimee and my gentleman in red velvets. I learned he was Aimee's cousin, Jacques de Sansard, the Bishop of Renne. He was only a few years over thirty, and in his hard eyes I spied the restless ambition that had lifted him to an important position at such a young age.

Ruby and sapphire rings flashed on his gloves as he spoke, and the family hung on his words. He included me in his conversation with easy courtesy, behaving as though our encounter on the stairs had never occurred.

After the meal, Aimee declared to her mother that she would take me to the salon of a redoubtable matron where the talk would be of moral plays. This surprised me, because Aimee's interest in moral plays about equaled her interest in plain boiled mutton. Once out of sight of her father's hôtel, however, Aimee bribed the coachman to silence — he seemed used to the procedure — and dragged me into a world of glittering decadence.

The fourteenth king Louis had reached middle age and life at court had grown a bit dull, but in Paris, the nobles still entertained themselves like spoilt and mischievous children. I had never seen this world of colorful salons, bright coins discretely changing hands, ladies and gentlemen promising sin with mere glances, but I knew my philandering husband had.

As Aimee whirled me from house to house, and I played the banned card game of *brelans* and ate ices and drank wine, I realized that Marcel had lived this life while I'd shivered in our rundown house wondering what I'd do when the next creditor banged on the door.

"I hope the fires are hot, Marcel," I muttered as I drained another goblet of wine.

"I beg your pardon, Madame?" the gentleman at my side at the *brelans* table asked. He put a hand on my waist. I tapped his arm with my fan and told him, with a smile, to behave himself.

The dancing, gaming, and flirting went on, but I was cautious by habit and stopped myself long before the night was over. I'd half expected one of the houses to be raided by the Paris police, led by one Pierre Marchand, a man wanting to rise in the world, who always thought me up to no good. Unfortunately, at times, he was right.

I'd learned that Monsieur Marchand had eleven children, which made me believe his struggle to rise through the ranks could not be an easy one. I once told him that a man bringing eleven children into the world ought to arrest *himself*. This was the first—and the only—time I had seen him smile.

I'd lost Aimee hours before, but I knew from experience she would turn up smiling and rosy and whisper to me of the gentleman or two she had conquered. I sent for Aimee's coach and instructed the coachman to take me to the Poullard house. He could return for Aimee while I put my already aching head to bed.

As the carriage rolled through a quiet avenue, a man staggered out of a side street and fell in front of the coach.

The coachman cursed, horses snorted, and the carriage careened sideways. I caught myself before I slid from the seat, then as the carriage rocked to a halt, I let down the window and peered out to see if the man had been hurt.

Below me on the drizzle-soaked cobbles, a man in red robes climbed to his feet and braced himself on the coach's wheel.

"Your Grace?" I asked in astonishment.

Jacques de Sansard looked up at me. His velvets were rumpled, his hair disheveled. His crucifix scattered blue radiance as it swung back and forth, the coach's light catching on the sapphires.

I opened the door. "You'd better get in."

The footman, recognizing the bishop, hopped from his perch and assisted him into the coach. The bishop collapsed onto the seat opposite me and lay against the cushions, breathing heavily. The footman slammed the door and the coach lurched onward.

"Your Grace," I said, keeping my voice soft.

He raised his head. As he had in the stairwell, he started then went still, his expression anguished. The next moment, he'd slid from the seat to his knees and buried his face in my lap. He grasped my hands with gloved fingers, and warm lips touched the inside of my wrist.

"Angél. You've come back to me."

I brushed back his sleek hair, my compassion stirring for this proud man who obviously grieved deeply. Jacques pressed a long kiss to my belly then, after a time, knelt back and looked up at me.

Uncertainty darkened his eyes. "You are not Angél."

"No. It's Émilie. I am sorry."

The bishop rested there, his hands on my skirts, as though not wanting to acknowledge his mistake, or to give up his vision.

"You loved her," I said gently.

A defiant blue sparkle worked through the confusion in his eyes. "I ought to be ashamed. But I am not."

I waited. In a moment, he went on. "Angél had nothing. I gave her all I could, but I could not give her the protection of my name. But my cousin Renaud needed a wife. I knew he would be good to her in his own way." The bishop's grip on my skirts tightened. "She was my life."

"Did you kill her?" I asked. In my experience, men who loved with passion often were the first the police turned to when the object of that love was killed.

The bishop straightened abruptly. "I loved her. I would never have hurt her." He levered himself from the floor and back onto his seat. "Why do you say *killed her*? It was an accident. She fell."

"Were you in the house when she died?" I asked, wondering how much he truly knew of what happened.

The bishop shook his head, tears shining on his face. "I was away. Madame Poullard wrote to me."

"I am sorry," I said again. He was hurting, this man, who could trust no one in his world of power and backbiting intrigue.

The bishop gave a negligent wave of his gloved hand. "It is no matter, Madame. I am not myself. I cannot think why I mistook you for …"

"You are befuddled with wine, Monsieur. As you said, not yourself."

My words seemed to relieve him. The bishop pulled out a handkerchief and sniffled into it, then he turned his face to the window and did not speak the rest of the way to the hôtel.

When Beatrice stripped my gown from me up in my chamber, I felt as though something heavy had been removed from my bones. Angel watched me from the wall, as though knowing I'd comforted her lover. Her smile was soft with gratitude.

Or so my wine-soaked thoughts told me. I crawled into the wide bed and slept deeply, and awoke with an aching head.

Aimee sent word next morning that she was ill—I could not wonder why—and would stay in bed all day. But the bishop had aroused my insatiable curiosity, and left on my own, I wandered the house, asking questions about Angél.

The servants responded readily enough, eager to impart the family tragedy.

"Right before my eyes, Madame," a ruddy-faced housemaid told me. "Madame Renaud rolled over the railing, all limp, her skirts fluttering like a bird's wings. Her head gave such a crack when she landed. I'll never forget it. I saw the blood, and I screamed and ran for help. But too late, I knew it."

The maid looked avid, not grieved, as though the death had happened to someone she hadn't known. All the servants behaved that way, however. Angél had been pretty and quiet, never had a row with her husband, they said, but no one knew much *about* her.

Later that afternoon I stitched silk embroidery in a salon with Aimee's oldest brother's wife, Léonore. Like the servants, Léonore Poullard showed no hesitation in discussing Angél.

"She was a quiet girl," Léonore said with a sniff. "Never said much for herself."

"How sad that she died," I responded, trying to sound polite and disinterested.

Léonore bit off a thread. "Indeed, it was sad. But accidents do happen. Renaud was able to marry Mathilde soon after, who is a much better wife to him. Angél was not suitable. I said as much to Jacques when he introduced them. I cannot know what Jacques was thinking."

She had little more to add. Léonore reiterated how much the family preferred the stolid and dependable Mathilde then turned the conversation to other topics.

After supper that night, I played piquet with Léonore's husband, Michel, a plump-faced man whose long black wig was a little too large for him. Michel also did not seem to find it unusual when I brought up the subject of Angél.

"She was a soft-spoken young woman." He paused to write down points for himself—thirty before we'd even played a trick, such was my bad luck. "But too pretty. She drew attention to herself."

I made the appropriate noise of sympathy for him having to witness such a thing. "You must have been shocked when she died."

"No, no, not shocked. We were surprised, naturally, but truth to tell, she was not happy, and I have always wondered if she didn't slip and fall on purpose. She was an odd creature and did not fit in with the rest of us."

I laid down a card. Everything I'd learned of Angél today had been unenlightening — she hadn't spoken much to the family, she hadn't fit in, she was not missed.

But the handsome, lively bishop had loved her. She must have had *something* in her, something that these dull, staid people had missed, and that Jacques de Sansard had understood.

I glanced up and found Renaud, Angél's husband, staring at me. I wondered if anyone could truly be as passionless as he appeared, and what kind of emotions, if any, lay behind his pale gaze.

I turned back to the game and found Michel also watching me, but in a different way. His gaze strayed to my décolletage, and his eyes betrayed his thoughts. I laid down another card, pretending not to notice.

Later, I drowsed in Angél's bed, the opiate I'd taken for my headache rendering me limp and tired. I lay with eyes half-closed and mulled over the maid's description of Angél's death.

I was certain of one thing. If *I* had tumbled over that railing I would never have gone limp and fallen without a peep. I would have screamed and flailed, desperate to save myself.

That suggested several things. First, that Angél had done away with herself as Michel would like to believe. That she'd been unhappy living in this house, I could well believe, but on the other hand, she only had to put up with the family until her bishop, a wealthy, intelligent, and handsome man, could come to her. I had no doubt that any gentleman who could rise to power as rapidly as Jacques would have canny ways to meet the woman he loved with no one being the wiser.

But people killed themselves for all sorts of reasons. I still hadn't made up my mind as to whether Angél had been truly happy.

Her death also might have been pure accident: Angél had fainted and fallen at a bad moment.

The third possibility was that someone had killed her. The upper hall was always badly lit, and the maid below might not have seen the person who'd pushed Angél to her death. Or Angél might have been killed elsewhere, and her body carried to the landing and dropped over.

On the other hand, most of the people in this house believed Angél's death had been nothing more than an unfortunate accident, even the bishop. Only I had my doubts, and my thoughts were reflected in the eyes of the woman staring at me from above the fireplace.

I groaned and rolled over. The opiate

made my limbs as loose as Angél's when she'd tumbled to her death. As I drifted to sleep, I again saw Michel's eyes, flat, brown, and filled with lust, then Renaud's blank, pig-like stare. Then the bishop's blue gaze: stern, terrible, grieving. I tried to shut them all away, but they followed me into my dreams.

The next day, my headache had gone. I spent the day shopping with Aimee and privately sifting through the puzzle of Angél's death. Aimee, also recovered, generously bought me a gown her dressmaker was trying to get rid of, and would not let me refuse it.

For supper I wore the new white and cream-colored silk and had Beatrice put up my hair to leave my neck bare. Aimee chattered and laughed throughout the meal, and the bishop, avoiding my eye, jested with her. Even Aimee's brothers and their wives let themselves be almost witty tonight.

In the salon, I played cards with Aimee's father and mother and Mathilde, Renaud's wife, and managed to win a few livres. Michel, at the next table, sent me suggestive glances whenever his wife's attention was elsewhere.

I rose early and announced I would retire. I paused by Michel's chair on my way to the door and let him catch my gaze. Mathilde, who also claimed fatigue, went upstairs with me, her tread heavy. We parted cordially on the landing, and I continued up another flight to my chamber.

Once there, I untied my hair and shook it down. I doused all but two candles the maid had left burning for me, fetched a bottle of wine and some goblets from the cupboard, and arranged everything on a round table with two chairs drawn up to it.

He didn't knock. He slipped into the room and closed the door, waiting for me to notice him. I waved him to one of the chairs and poured wine, dark and red, into a goblet.

"You are beautiful tonight, Madame." He seated himself, took up his goblet, and drank noisily. When he set the glass down, a red droplet clung to his mouth.

"Thank you. I am glad you like me this way. I took the idea from Angél." I gestured to the portrait.

His brows drew down, and he turned to look up at the painting. While his attention was on the portrait, I moved quickly to his chair. I'd positioned the candles so their glare was behind me, and my shadow fell upon him.

He gazed at the painting for a long moment, then turned back to me, starting when he saw me over him.

Color drained from his face. "Dear God."

He reached out an uncertain finger and touched the lace on my skirt. "Angél?"

"Do you remember?" I asked in a quiet voice.

His finger shook, and he withdrew it. "No."

"You remember." I went on relentlessly. He knew what had happened, damn him, but I had to make him tell me. "Here in this room. You found Angél, asleep on her bed."

He nodded, his eyes half closing. "She thought I was Jacques."

"But she said nothing."

Michel's faced flushed with sudden rage. "She did not. But why shouldn't I have her, Jacques' whore? He brought her here under our noses, and my brother was completely blind. Angél let me touch her. She should not have, but she let me without making a sound."

"Because she was afraid of you," I said, my voice hardening. "You killed her because you feared she would tell Jacques. You put something in the wine, an opiate perhaps, something strong enough to make her sleep and never wake. Then you carried her to the stairs and dropped her over."

Michel clenched his fists on the table — large beefy fists that could knock me to the floor. "No."

"I asked for an opiate yesterday. A good,

strong dose for my headache. All of it is in your glass."

Michel stared at his nearly empty goblet, his face draining of color. He pushed me away, his jaw slack. I smiled.

Michel lunged for me, but he was clumsy with drink, and I'd already moved. I was across the bedchamber before Michel could struggle to his feet. I wrenched open the door … and collided with Jacques de Sansard who rushed into the room, eyes blazing like the sapphires on his crucifix.

"You killed her, Michel." His voice cut like falling ice. "I've always believed so. May God have mercy on your soul."

The rest of the Poullard family straggled into the antechamber in response to the noise. Mathilde, dressed for bed, huddled in her dressing gown.

Michel thrust a pleading hand at them. "Help me. She's given me poison to drink. Angél has killed me."

"Nonsense," I said crisply. "I am Émilie, and I have given you nothing but wine."

For a moment, Michel stared in choked silence, then he howled and leapt at me. The bishop seized him and bore him to the floor.

Monsieur Poullard cleared his throat, looking embarrassed. A cool father indeed, who could only respond with shame that his son was a murderer. Or perhaps he'd suspected, had made his peace with it long ago. "Please take him away, Jacques."

Michel's wife, Léonore, peered over her father-in-law's shoulder. Her face was white, her dark eyes wide, but she made no move, voiced no protest.

Jacques hauled Michel to his feet. I closed my eyes to shut out the bishop's cold and merciless face as he dragged Michel past.

Michel been the only one of the household to show any interest in common desire — even Jacques knew how to hide his emotions. Only when Jacques had been confused by me in the shadows, or befuddled with drink, had he shown his true self, and he'd pulled his mask into place very quickly.

Michel, a man who enjoyed lusts, married to a rather passionless wife, would have found the pretty Angél irresistible. And why not? he would think. Angél had been his brother's wife, but the lover of his cousin — why should he not enjoy what she obviously gave freely?

I knew that, once arrested, Michel's fate would be swift: interrogation, torture, imprisonment, execution. A man with the power of Jacques de Sansard could extract a brutal and final vengeance.

When I opened my eyes again, I found only Monsieur Poullard and Renaud left in the antechamber — Mathilde, Madame

Poullard, and Aimee must have taken Léonore away. The two men looked at me uneasily and then at each other, as though uncertain what to do. I doubted anything so scandalous had ever happened in their stoic lives.

I closed the door on them, not caring if I were rude. I leaned against the bedchamber door, wretched and weak, hearing the drip, drip, drip of scarlet wine falling from goblet to carpet.

"I hope you are finished, Angél," I said softly.

From somewhere a faint whisper touched me — a breath, a sigh — then it was gone.

I longed suddenly for the chaos and noise of Versailles and the court, for the tantrums of Madame de Montespan, the petty games of the courtiers and their ladies, the splendor of Louis' gardens. A colorful and lively world compared to this quiet house where people lived oblivious to its luxuries, where those who did not belong came to a tragic end. Only Aimee seemed untouched, but then she had escaped at a young age, and was now more a product of the court than this stolid, wealthy family.

Someone tapped on the bedchamber door. I roused myself and opened it to find the bishop, still in his velvets, on the threshold. He looked at me in my white silk, then past me at the portrait over the mantel. When his gaze came back to me his eyes held caution and a bit of respect.

He gave me a bow. "Thank you, Madame."

I spread my hands. "I did nothing."

Jacques's mouth set. "You found out what truly happened to the woman I loved. Michel murdered her, and he will pay. I will always be grateful to you." He paused, looking me up and down again. "I am very rich, Madame. I can offer you a reward for this deed."

I swallowed. At court, I had to fend for myself, finding my own meals, paying for every expense. Madame de Montespan could have fits of generosity, and would not leave me entirely destitute, but much of the time, I lived on a pittance.

But such money would always remind me of Angél, of Michel's blaze of lust, of Jacques' anguish when he crushed my hands between his in the darkness of the carriage.

"No," I said. "Thank you. I do not want it."

Jacques looked surprised, but seemed to understand, and gave me a nod. "As you wish. If you change your mind, you may write to me."

I didn't answer. Jacques looked at me for a long moment, then he leaned forward and pressed a brief kiss to my lips. Then he turned away, and was gone.

I closed the door and gazed up at Angél. The painted woman's smile seemed a little wider, and the light in her eyes matched what I'd seen in the bishop's when he'd thrown Michel to the floor.

I put out the last of my candles and drowned the portrait in darkness.

I never heard anything of Michel Poullard after that. But weeks later, after I had returned to Versailles, I learned that Jacques de Sansard had been given a second bishopric. Gossip said his power was on the rise to even greater heights.

I saw Jacques once after that, a year later, in an avenue in Paris. Astride a fine horse, surrounded by retainers, his costly cloak adorned with a bejeweled brooch, Jacques swept a stern gaze about him, his look powerful and proud. If he saw me, he made no acknowledgment.

But I remembered his head on my lap, his tears wetting my skin as he grieved for a pretty young girl taken from him too soon.

After my visit to Aimee, my life at court went on as usual — that is to say, I was surrounded by gossip, intrigue, and squabbles both petty and serious.

Madame de Montespan welcomed me back, telling me she hoped I wouldn't make a habit of running off to Paris when she and the dear queen needed me so much. I settled into my routine of brushing the queen's dogs, fetching the queen's gloves, delivering secret notes for Montespan, and avoiding the attention of Louis the king as much as I could. Louis had discovered my talent for ferreting out information, and used me from time to time to help him with problems he wanted no one else to know about. Thankfully, he did not seem to need my services for now, and so my life was tranquil, at least as much at it could be in the court of the Sun King.

Pierre Marchand, the policeman, got word of the arrest in Paris and my hand in it. He stopped me as I strolled the market in Versailles one evening, purchasing food for my meager supper.

Monsieur Marchand was a tall man, in his thirties, with fair hair, a high forehead, and a nose that was long and sloping. He never bothered with a wig and often tied his hair back to keep it out of his way. He was not handsome but his brown eyes held something as lively and confident as Jacques's blue ones had.

I found the butt of Pierre's walking stick stopping my foot as I turned away from one of the vendors. He did not need this stick to support himself—he preferred to terrify criminals with it.

Pierre gave me a shallow bow, but did not move the stick. "You cause trouble, Madame, it seems, wherever you go."

I tried to shrug as I tucked my dinner of pullet and bread securely away inside my cloak. "It was not I who caused the trouble, Monsieur. I was simply sorry for the young woman who did not fit in."

"And a respectable family felt the touch of scandal."

"The scandal was not mine," I said indignantly. "I merely exposed it."

Marchand only looked at me, those shrewd eyes of his seeing everything. "You are a dangerous woman, Madame d'Armand."

"So you have said. May I get on? Or have you come to arrest me for purchasing slightly overdone pullet?"

Pierre never smiled, as I said, but I saw a spark of amusement in his eyes. "I would have done the same, had I been there. In my own way, of course."

He would. Perhaps I'd been learning too many of his tricks. Pierre bowed to me and strolled away, and the vendor selling the chicken in sauce sighed in relief. Marchand had a reputation as a policeman who always got his man—or woman—no matter how many people he had to arrest before he found the right culprit.

I watched Pierre walk away, his tied-back hair swaying across his dark coat, his head turning so his keen eye could watch for any wrongdoing. He technically only held power in Paris, but this did not stop him from ferreting out crime wherever he went.

I returned to my shopping, hoping I'd heard the last of a matter I longed to put behind me.

The white gown I never wore again. I instructed Beatrice to sell it, and I distributed the proceeds to the beggars.

End

A Soupçon of Poison

A Soupçon of Poison

A Kat Holloway Mystery

Chapter One

London, 1880

I am a cook, and better than most, even at my young age of nine and twenty, and the gentry and aristocracy pay highly to have me.

Sir Lionel Leigh-Bradbury of Portman Square gave me less than I might have had elsewhere, but when the agency told me he'd agreed to the large number of days out a month I'd requested, I leapt at the position.

I had never actually met Sir Lionel—the housekeeper and the agency made all the negotiations with me—until I'd been in his employ nearly two months. Then, one evening, he abruptly summoned me.

Copley, the thin, sour-faced butler with a walleye, delivered the news to the kitchen. "'Is royal 'ighness demands your presence. In 'is library."

I stilled my knife on the carcass of an onion spread before me. *"Now?"* I asked crossly.

I had much work to prepare for supper, having no assistant. Sir Lionel employed only one footman and a scullery maid in addition to housekeeper, butler, and cook. He kept the housekeeper and butler only because he'd inherited them with the house and title.

Copley banged down his salver and threw himself into a chair by the fire. "No," he snarled. "'E must 'ave meant in a fortnight."

Copley despised all women in general and me in particular. He was pinch-faced, bad-tempered and usually half drunk with gin.

I began chopping again, with more vigor this time. "He stays above stairs, and I stay below," I said. "It is the proper way of things."

"Am I to blame for 'is upbringing? You'd best get to it, woman."

I sighed, finished the onion, and carefully washed my knife before putting it away. Onion juice left to dry can be disastrous to cutlery. I put the onions in a bowl, wiped my hands, and went to face my employer for the first time.

Sir Lionel sat alone in the library on the second floor. The high-ceilinged, dark-beamed room was cold, musty, and dimly lit. Tall bookcases lined the room, each packed so tightly with books I doubted that any could be pried out and actually read.

My employer reposed at a writing table with about a dozen photographs on it. As I came as close as I dared, I saw that the photos were of older Leigh-Bradburys, of Sir Lionel in formal dress, and one of a young woman, pretty, whom I did not recognize. That photo looked old, but the frame was new, so perhaps it was a beloved sister or beau who had passed away.

Sir Lionel had limp brown hair that hung from a bald place on top of his head, a white face, and a long nose. His limbs were almost as thin as Copley's, and his long coat hung on his bony shoulders. He was middle-aged and had recently inherited this house, all its contents, and his baronetcy from his uncle.

I stopped a foot or so from the desk and folded my hands on my plump abdomen. "You asked to see me, sir?"

Sir Lionel looked me up and down, his prominent Adam's apple moving. "*You* are my cook?"

I inclined my head. "I am Mrs. Holloway, sir."

"*Mrs.* Holloway." He leaned forward a little as he said the name. "You are married?"

My matrimonial state was none of his business. "All cooks are called missus, sir," I said stiffly.

Sir Lionel continued to stare at me, his blue eyes so wide they protruded. The good Lord had blessed me with a comely face—so I'd been told—a mass of curling dark hair, and a figure that was curved and not angular, but I saw no reason for such amazement.

"You sent for me, sir," I prompted as Sir Lionel continued to stare at me.

"Oh. Yes. I wanted to … I wanted …" He trailed off and assumed a fretful frown. "I am feeling unwell. The dish you prepared for my supper last night is to blame."

"The cassoulet?" I said in surprise. "Of course it was not to blame. Everyone in this house partook of that dish, and no one has any ill effects. It was perfectly fine."

"It tasted off."

"Nonsense. The chicken was freshly killed and the vegetables fine and crisp. I was lucky to get them and at a fair price."

Sir Lionel tapped the arms of his chair. "I have eaten only your cassoulet since last night, and I am ill. What else could it be?"

I eyed him critically. "If you've eaten naught else, it's no wonder you're ill. I'll make you a cup of beef tea, sir, and send you up some seedcake."

He looked indignant. "I do not want—"

"Certainly you do," I interrupted. "Your humors are out of balance and need some easing. I ate a good portion of that cassoulet, and as you can see, I am fit and hale. You want a bit of grub in your belly, that is all."

Sir Lionel gave me a dazed look, as though not used to being told what to do, even if it was for his own good. "Er, yes, quite. Yes, yes, send it up, whatever you like."

I gave him a little bow and turned away, feeling his gaze on my back all the way to the door.

Downstairs, I cut up seedcake and fixed a thick broth of beef with black pepper. I set this all on a tray, which was carried upstairs by the footman, because Copley was snoring and unlikely to rouse himself the rest of the night.

My cakes seemed to have done the trick, as did my supper of thick slices of pork, hearty bread, and onion soup, for I heard no more complaints about illness and no more words against my cooking. I did not see Sir Lionel again for another three weeks.

Late one night, after the other staff had gone to bed, I sat in the kitchen at the wide wooden table, sharpening my knives.

A cook's knives are her greatest asset, and if they go dull, they are no use at all and should be replaced. As decent knives are hideously expensive, I kept mine in good repair.

I did not trust anyone with the task of sharpening but myself, so I sat on my stool, alone, and drew a blade across the damped stone. The only sound in the silent room was the scrape of stone on steel and the hiss of the oil lamp beside me.

The solitude comforted me. I'd had a trying day. Copley's bunions had played him up, making him more sour than usual, and he'd gone so far as to throw a bowl of porridge at me. John the footman had dropped and shattered a crock full of sugar. The scullery maid had taken sick, so I'd had to do all the washing up myself.

Because of that, by the time I'd gotten to the market, all the best produce was gone. My bread had over-risen and deflated upon itself while I was out because John had been too stupid to follow the simplest instructions.

I'd made my disapprobation known, and the others had retired somewhat earlier than usual, leaving me alone with my knives.

Where Sir Lionel found me.

"Mrs. Holloway?"

I peered through the kitchen's gloom, my comfort evaporating. The master of the house stood at the door to the stairway, his breathing loud and hoarse. He moved across the flagstones to the table where I sat, and gazed at me with eyes that were sunken and petulant.

I jumped to my feet, annoyed. The kitchen was my demesne. The master might own the house, but a good employer understood that not interfering in the kitchen made for a tranquil domestic situation. Sir Lionel had his rooms above stairs where I did not trespass, and he had no reason to trespass on *me*.

"Might I help you with something, sir?" I asked, striving to remain polite.

"Good heavens, Mrs. Holloway." Sir Lionel, his voice breathy, looked past me at the table. "What is it you're doing?"

Dancing naked upon Hampstead Heath. "Just giving my knives a bit of attention, sir. I like them nice and sharp."

"Yes, I am certain you do."

Before I could decipher this comment, Sir Lionel had moved abruptly to my side and pinned me against the table. He was stronger than his size let on, and he held me fast with his spindly arms.

"Mrs. Holloway, I can think of nothing but you. Of your eyes, your hair …" He pulled a lock free from my cap. "Your bosom, so comely. Do you have children?"

"One," I gasped, the truth I kept hidden bursting out in my amazement.

He did not seem to hear me. "My nursery maid had a bosom as large as yours. She let me feast upon her."

I scarcely wanted to think about *that*. I desperately craned my head away from his port-laden breath and bloodshot eyes.

"Let me feast upon you, Katharine."

Oh, this would never do. I groped behind me across the smooth boards of the table and closed my fingers around the handle of a knife.

It was my carver. I pulled it around and brought it up right under Sir Lionel's chin.

Sir Lionel squeaked in alarm. His gaze shot to the knife then back to me, spots of red burning on his cheeks. He must have seen something in my blue eyes he so admired, because he released me and took a hasty step backward.

"Sir," I said in a hard voice. "You employ me and pay my wages. I cook. That line should *never* be crossed."

Sir Lionel's mouth opened and closed a few times. "It should not?"

"No, sir. It should not."

His petulant look returned. "But you are so beautiful."

I held the knife point steady, though I was shaking all the way through. "You flatter me, sir. I am a cook, is all. You go along upstairs and to bed. You will feel better in the morning."

"No, no ...er. I am going out."

"Right, then, sir. Off you go."

Sir Lionel eyed the glinting knife blade, stared at my bosom with stark regret, turned on his heel, and marched out of the room.

Not until I'd heard him tramp all the way up the stairs and slam the door above did I let out an explosive breath and drop to the stool, the strength gone out of me.

"Fool," came a voice.

I smothered a yelp as Copley materialized from the shadows. My knife clattered to the table.   "What the devil do you mean, skulking about like that?" I cried.

Copley gave me a sickly grin, his walleye gleaming. "Ye could 'ave gained some favors with 'im, woman. You give 'im a bit, and 'e gives you a rise in wages. Any sensible woman would think it a bit of luck."

"I *am* a sensible woman," I said firmly. "Which is why I told him to be gone."

"Maybe 'e'd even marry you." Copley sniggered, a dry sound.

"Oh, most like. The gentry don't marry cooks." Thank heavens. On the other hand, I might have just lost myself my post.

Copley scooted close enough to me that I could smell the gin on his breath. "I'll keep this atween you and me. Can't let it get about that you cast your eyes upon the master, can it?"

He'd turn it about and spread that story, simply because he could. "You are a little swine," I said. "I did nothing of the sort."

"But none know it but me, you, and 'is nibs, do they? And I seed 'ow quick you was to shove a knife at 'is throat."

"I only meant to frighten him." I let my tone grow chilly. "I thought it most effective. Didn't you?"

Copley's gaze slid to the knife that rested near my hand, and he faded back from me. "I'll remember it. I will." And thankfully, he shuffled away, heading upstairs to his bed.

I went back to sharpening the blades that had done me so much good tonight, but it was a long time before I could stop shaking. Longer still before I could make myself retire to my tiny bedchamber tucked behind the kitchen and sleep.

***

The next day, Daniel McAdam came whistling down the kitchen steps to deliver a bushel of apples.

Daniel McAdam had, as we ladies put it, a way with him. I'd known him for about a year, ever since the day he'd stepped into old Mrs. Pauling's kitchens, where'd I'd formerly worked, to get out of the rain. Daniel ever after paused to flirt with me, harmless like, whenever he made a delivery to Mrs. Pauling's house, and now to Sir Lionel's.

I knew little about Daniel, even after a year. He was a man of all work and a jack of all trades. He delivered goods, carried messages, and ran far and wide about London—once I'd seen him driving a hired carriage, competently maneuvering it through the crowds.

I did not know where he lodged or where he disappeared to for weeks at a time. He'd only wink and answer evasively whenever I brought up these subjects.

I knew Daniel wasn't married because I'd asked him that, point blank. When a man flirts with a woman, she ought to know where things stand.

Daniel had dark hair and dark eyes and a tall, attractive body. He spoke with a fairly neutral accent—he hadn't been brought up on the streets, I could tell. He could read and write and was quite clever, though he never admitted to any schooling.

I concluded that he must be the son of a middle-class gentleman, possibly illegitimate, but he never spoke of his family. He turned his hand to a good many menial tasks, things even a destitute gentleman might shun, which was why I thought him a bastard son. Father genteel, mother a tavern maid or something of the sort, and now Daniel had to grub for a living.

No matter who he was, Daniel seemed to be happy puttering about London, making friends with everyone he met and doing any odd job he could.

It was a daft way to live, and I told him so. He only laughed and said: *Some of us were born to work and others to keep the devil amused.*

He always said something nonsensical when he did not want to give an answer.

This morning, Daniel set down the apples and waited with good humor while I wiped my hands of puff pastry dough and poured him a cup of steaming tea.

Daniel swallowed a long drink and grinned at Copley, who leaned against the wall, barely able to stand. "You'll kill yourself with gin, Copley." Daniel took a flask from his pocket and dropped a dollop of whiskey into his own cup.

Copley gave him a sour look. He'd woken with a raging headache and had been sick in the basin twice already. "I were up late. Woke by the master and Mrs. Holloway a'carrying on, weren't I?"

Daniel raised dark brows. I dumped a large ball of butter onto my dough and vigorously attacked the mess with my rolling pin.

"Why don't you tell 'im, Mrs. H?" Copley

rasped. "About 'ow the master tried it on with you, and ye almost slit 'is throat?"

Chapter Two

Daniel did not change expression, but his black gaze focused on me. "What happened, Kat?" he asked, his tone gentle.

Daniel was the only person I allowed to call me *Kat*. Not that I'd given him permission. He'd simply taken it up, and I'd not prevented him.

I rolled the pastry dough flat and used my scraper to fold each third in on itself before going at it again. Puff pastry was difficult to get right, and a kitchen full of curious people was not assisting me to concentrate.

"Nothing as interesting as Copley makes out," I said crisply.

"Even so, tell me."

When Daniel McAdam spoke in that voice — quiet and friendly, yet full of steel, people tended to obey him. I stopped pounding at the dough, which needed to rest and cool anyway, and gave him an abbreviated account of the incident. Copley snorted a few times and inserted foolish comments at intervals.

Daniel helped himself to another cup of tea, minus the whiskey this time, and sipped it as I talked. When I finished, Daniel rose from the stool where he'd been sitting and set the cup on the draining board by the sink. "Copley," he said in that steely voice. "A word, if you please."

Copley looked surprised, but as I said, people tended to obey Daniel without quite knowing why.

Copley followed Daniel across the kitchen and out the scullery door. The scullery maid, sniffling with her cold, let dirty water drip all over the flagstone floor while she watched Daniel with lovesick eyes.

I have no idea to this day what Daniel said to Copley, but when Copley returned he was subdued. He skulked across the kitchen without looking at me and stomped up the stairs.

***

The very next morning Sir Lionel started taking his vengeance on me for not only rejecting his advances but putting my knife to his throat. He did nothing so direct as sack me—oh, no. He went about it by more subtler means, trying to vanquish me, if you like.

Now, you may wonder why I did not simply pack up my knives and march out, but while good cooks are in demand, good places aren't all that thick on the ground. As horrible as Sir Lionel was, he lived in London, where I needed to stay, the wage was decent, and I had my many days out a month, which was the most important thing to me. So I stayed and put up with him.

Sir Lionel did not come to the kitchen again—he'd learned that lesson. He sent his demands through Mrs. Watkins, the housekeeper. Sometimes Copley delivered the messages, but even Sir Lionel realized that Copley couldn't be trusted when he was befuddled with drink, so Mrs. Watkins brought down most of his orders.

Mrs. Watkins had worked in this house for many years, previously for Sir Lionel's uncle, and she didn't think much of the current master. She was straight-backed and pinch-nosed and set in her ways, and didn't hold with all this cooking nonsense—a bit of boiled mutton was all a body needed, and any simpleton could buy that in a shop. For all her decided opinions, Mrs. Watkins wasn't a bad sort, although she didn't approve of cooks being as young as I was.

I couldn't help my age—I'd been assistant to one of the best cooks in London at fifteen, and had proved to have a talent for the job. That cook had passed on when I'd been twenty, word had spread that her apprentice could replicate her meals, and agencies fought to have me on their books.

However, I had to be choosy where I worked, and my situation with Sir Lionel, unfortunately, was ideal. Except for Sir Lionel, of course. Mrs. Watkins made it plain that Sir Lionel was a disappointment after his uncle, who'd been a true gentleman, she said, but Mrs. Watkins, like me, needed the position.

Sir Lionel began his game of revenge by sending down odd and impossible requests for his dinners—wild birds that wouldn't be in season for another few months, tender vegetables that had gone out of season months before, and dishes even I had never heard of. I had to read through my treasured tomes to find recipes for what he wanted, and some I simply had to invent. Even the exhaustive Mrs. Beeton failed me from time to time.

Some days I'd nearly make myself ill getting the meal finished to his order—I had my pride, after all—and he'd send word at the last minute that he would dine at his club and wouldn't be back until morning.

The delicate meal wouldn't keep for a day, so I and the household staff ate it. I had to watch John the footman bolt my coq a vin like it was mutton stew and listen to Mrs. Watkins complain that food should be simple without all this fuss. Copley would eat steadily, then follow the meal with a mug of gin and belch loudly.

The morning after, Sir Lionel would send down a sternly worded note that I'd spent far too much money on foodstuffs and threaten to take it out of my wages.

A lesser cook would have fled. But it built up my pride that I was mostly able to fulfill his bizarre requests and build a meal around them, no matter how much Sir Lionel made clear he did not appreciate it. I rose to the challenge, wanting to prove he could not best me.

Where he came up with his ideas for what he wanted me to cook I had no idea. Sir Lionel did not strike me as a refined gentleman with cultivated tastes. Likely he found descriptions of dishes in books, or he had a friend who made up the meals for him, laughing about the good trick they were playing on a cook who needed to learn her place.

Then came the day I nearly threw down my apron and ran out the door to never come back. Mrs. Watkins, at seven o'clock in the evening, brought me down a note telling me he wanted truffles a l'Italienne with beef in pepper sauce that night.

"Truffles?" I bellowed. "Where does he think I will find a handful of black truffles at this time of day?"

"I couldn't say." It was obvious Mrs. Watkins had no idea what a truffle was. "But he is adamant."

It was impossible. I knew all the good markets and who might have decent exotic fungi, but I had no time to get to them before they shut up for the night.

As luck would have it, an urchin I'd seen helping Daniel unload his goods a time or two was hanging around the scullery door. He'd been hoping for scraps or a chat with the scullery maid, but I stormed out to him, seized him by the ear, and told him to find Daniel for me.

"Scour the town if you must," I said. "Tell him Mrs. Holloway desperately needs his help. There's tuppence in it for you if you hurry."

The urchin jerked himself from me and rubbed his ear, but he didn't look angry. "Don't worry, missus. I'll find 'im."

The lad was true to his word. Daniel came knocking within the hour, and the lad happily jingled the coins I dropped into his hand.

Daniel listened to me rant, his warm smile nearly enough to calm my troubles. Nearly. When I finished, Daniel held out his hand.

"Give me your list, and I'll find the things for you," he said.

"How can you?" My voice rose, tinged with hysteria. "In half an hour?"

Daniel only regarded me calmly as he took the paper upon which I'd written ingredients. "The sooner I am gone, the sooner I can return."

I let out my breath, my heart in my words. "Thank you. I don't know who you are, Daniel McAdam, but you are a godsend."

Something flickered in his dark blue eyes, but his crooked smile returned. "I've been called much worse, Kat, believe me. Back in a tick."

He did return very quickly with a bundle of all I needed, including the finest truffles I'd ever seen and a small bottle of champagne, which Sir Lionel never stocked in his cellar. I did not like to ask how Daniel had come by the rarer things, and he did not volunteer the information.

Daniel tried to refuse money for the foodstuffs. He held his up his hands, spreading his fingers wide. "It was a challenge, Kat. I never knew the intricacies of food purchasing or how many markets we have in London. Keep your money for the next meal he demands."

"Don't talk nonsense. I'll not take them as gifts. Stand there while I get you some coin."

I hurried down to the housekeeper's parlor where we kept a locked tin of cash on hand for extra expenses. Only I and Mrs. Watkins had the key to it—Copley couldn't be trusted not to spend the money on drink.

Daniel hadn't given me a tally, but I counted out what I thought would be the cost of the goods and rushed back out, to find Daniel nowhere in sight.

"Where is Mr. McAdam?" I asked the urchin, who'd remained to make sheep's eyes at the scullery maid.

"'E's off," the urchin answered. "Said 'e couldn't wait."

"Blast the man," I said fervently.

I put the money back into the tin but vowed I'd force it upon him somehow one day. A woman couldn't afford to have a man do her expensive favors, especially a man as beguiling as Daniel McAdam. I'd learned all about the dangers of pretty men at a very young age, and I'd had enough of *that*.

***

Sir Lionel's next unreasonable dinner demand came the very next day. He decided, at five o'clock, if you please, that he'd entertain friends at his dinner table at seven. Mrs. Watkins brought down the order and stepped back as I read it.

Leek and cream soup, whitefish in a velouté sauce, green salad, squab stuffed with peppercorns, beef in a wine sauce, asparagus with egg, fricassee of wild mushrooms, soft rolls, a chocolate soup and a berry tart for pudding.

"Has he gone mad?" I screeched. "I haven't a scrap of chocolate in the house, no hope of fresh fish or game birds today." I flung the paper to the table. "That is the last straw, Mrs. Watkins. Either we come to an understanding or I give my notice. I ought to simply give it now and leave, let him and his guests do with salt pork and potatoes."

Copley, lounging in his chair near the fire, cackled. "Mrs. H. can't do it. All I hear is what a grand cook she is, how everyone wants her, how she's wasted in this 'ouse. She's asked to cook a few bits of fish, and she 'as hysterics. If you're so sought after, my girl, why ain't ye cooking for dukes, or for one of the royals?"

I dragged in a breath, trying to ignore Copley. "I agree that if I can pull this meal together it would make my reputation. But . . . oh—"

"Would it?" Mrs. Watkins picked up the list again, which she'd written in her careful hand at Sir Lionel's dictation. "I confess, I've never heard of velouté or eaten chocolate soup."

"Well, you shall eat it tonight. You, Mr. Copley, can cease laughing at me and help. I shall need a good bottle of sweet white wine and a robust red for the beef sauce and the chocolate. A claret for the table. *Asparagus* — I ask you. Any I can find will be woody and tasteless. But perhaps . . ." I trailed off, my inventive mind taking over.

"Ye can't be wanting *three* bottles," Copley said, sitting up. "The master comes over snarling if I open more than one a day."

"If he wants this food and wants it done well, he'll not quibble."

Copley scowled, unhappy, but he stomped away to fetch what I needed. I always thought it a mercy Copley found wine sour and without a good kick or Sir Lionel's wine collection, a fine one built up by his uncle, would be long gone.

"How many at table?" I asked Mrs. Watkins.

"Three," she said, folding her hands. Her long string of keys hung from her belt like a jailer's. "The master and two guests, a Mr. and Mrs. Fuller."

"At least he didn't invite twenty," I said. "Small blessings, I suppose." I scanned the kitchen, and sure enough, found Daniel's lad and the scullery maid outside together on the steps.

"*You*," I called to the youth from the back

door—I really ought to learn his name. "If you find Mr. McAdam for me in half an hour, this time I'll give you a shilling."

The boy grinned, saluted me, and off he went.

Chapter Three

Daniel came in twenty minutes. I explained my predicament, and again, he showed no qualms about searching the city for all I needed.

"How can you?" I asked, handing him the list I'd written out. "I *could* find all this, if I had a day or two."

Daniel shrugged. His dark hair was spotted with rain, which had begun to fall hard. Perhaps we'd have a flood, and Sir Lionel's guests wouldn't be able to come.

"My deliveries take me all over London," Daniel said. "I know who has what, who can get what."

He spoke easily, as though producing expensive foodstuffs out of the air was nothing. "What on earth do you deliver?" I asked.

Another shrug. "This and that." Daniel winked, actually tweaked my nose, and then disappeared up the stairs, whistling.

"That man is trouble," Mrs. Watkins said darkly, folding her arms as she watched him go.

"Daniel? I mean, Mr. McAdam?" I quickly turned to start scrubbing down my work table. "He's a kind soul, is all."

"Hmph." Mrs. Watkins made a motion of dusting off her hands. "I say trouble. Well, I must get on making sure the house is to rights. Sally!" she shouted at the scullery maid. "Get in here and wash up those dishes, girl, or I'll take a strap to you."

***

Daniel returned more quickly than I'd thought he could. I was in the butler's pantry, arguing with Copley about the wine, when Daniel arrived, dumped several boxes next to my work table, and disappeared again.

Copley did know a surprising amount about wine, which explained why he kept his post as butler, plus he could put on a toffy accent for the guests when he chose. I finally came away with a decent German Riesling and a deep red Côtes du Rhône, with his promise to decant the best of the claret.

By the time I emerged, Daniel had come

and gone. I was disappointed not to speak to him, but I was soon too busy to think more about it.

Daniel had brought me everything I needed, even fresh fish. They were perfectly fine, firm, slick, with no fishy smell to clog up the kitchen.

Now to prepare all these dishes in no time at all, including a white sauce that needed to simmer, and make feather-light rolls to go with everything.

If I'd been in a larger household, with several assistants, I could do this meal in a trice. As it was, I was soon in despair. The fish had to be cleaned, the fowls plucked and readied, the vegetables scrubbed and chopped. The velouté had to be constantly stirred so the delicate thickened stock didn't burn, the tart shells formed, chilled, and baked. I gave vent to my feelings, which only sent everyone else running away, leaving me on my own.

Almost. As I was up to my arms in fish entrails, the urchin came tripping into the kitchen without so much as a by-your-leave.

"I don't have any more errands for you," I said to him in irritation.

The lad, not cowed, didn't leave. "Mr. McAdam sent me. He says whatever you need help with, I was to do, even if it were cooking."

I stared at him in surprise. He was a sturdy young man, about fifteen, I'd say, with strong-looking hands. He was also filthy.

"John!" I bellowed. The footman popped his head around the corner from the servants' hall, where he was frantically polishing silver. I pointed my bloody fillet knife at the urchin. "Get him cleaned up and lend him some clothes. You can't come near this kitchen, lad, until all that dirt is off you. No one wants fleas in their dinner. Make sure he scrubs his hair, John. With soap."

John nodded solemnly, the urchin sent me a grin, and both youths were off.

When the urchin returned, he was urchin no longer. Now that his hair was clean, I saw it gleam dark red. His face was freckled, a fact I hadn't been able to detect under the grime, and his eyes were clear and brown. He had even teeth and good breath, and he'd trimmed his nails and scrubbed under them. John had lent him some trousers, shirt, and coat, all of which were a bit tight, but he'd do.

"What's your name?" I asked him.

The lad shrugged, an imitation of Daniel's. "You can call me James."

Which meant that might or might not be his name, but I had no time to quibble. "Very well, James, I need you to prepare this fowl for me. Here's how you do it . . ."

James proved quite competent. I could tell he'd never done any cookery before, but he was a quick learner, and worked steadily, without idle chatter or asking useless questions. Between the two of us, I prepared a meal a duchess would swoon over.

Perhaps I *would* seek out a duchess, one who stayed in town much of the time, and show her what fine dishes I could contrive.

But the main reason I did not seek out a society hostess was because working in smaller houses for bachelors like Sir Lionel meant I had much time to myself. Not today, obviously, but most of the time. A cook working for a duchess who had dinner parties every day would be laboring from dawn to midnight, never mind how many underlings she had. I had reason to want to come and go as often as I could, and so I stayed in houses like this one.

The finished meal did me proud. I thanked James profusely, asked him to sup with the rest of us, and happily gave him a few more shillings. The dishes went up to the dining room via the lift in the corner, and Mrs. Watkins saw that all was served.

Why not Copley? Because he'd fled the house while I had been ordering everyone about in the kitchen, got roaring drunk, and collapsed when he finally came back in. John and James carried him off to bed, which left Mrs. Watkins and John to see to the dining room. Mrs. Watkins was angry at this turn of events, but I knew she'd manage.

Every plate came back scraped clean. My pride puffed up. They'd loved it.

I was, as far as I was concerned that night, the greatest cook in the land.

***

It was late before I crawled off, exhausted, to seek my bed. My bedroom was a cubby-hole of a chamber, but I liked it because it lay right behind the kitchen fireplace, which kept it warm and dry.

I was deep in the slumber of the just when the scullery maid, Sally, shook me awake into darkness. "Oh, Mrs. Holloway," she said breathlessly. "There's someone above stairs."

I screwed my eyes shut against the flickering flame of her candle. "Of course there's someone above stairs. Likely his royal highness stumbling to bed after drinking himself into a stupor."

"No, ma'am. It ain't Sir Lionel." Sally regarded me in terror. "The guests left hours ago, and the master dragged 'imself off to bed already. It ain't John or Copley neither. I 'eard 'em snoring when I passed their rooms. And Mrs. Watkins went off to visit her sister."

I levered myself to a sitting position. I did

not ask why Sally hadn't woken the men instead of trotting all the way downstairs to me. Copley and John would be useless and we both knew it.

"Get the poker then, girl. If it's burglars, we'll set about them."

Sally's eyes grew even more round. I threw back the covers and swung my feet to the floor, pressing them into my slippers. Sally scuttled into the kitchen and wrested the poker from its place with so much clanking I was sure the thieves would hear and run away directly.

I didn't bother with my knives. They were suited to hacking chickens, chopping onions, and frightening overly amorous masters. For fending off marauders, a poker or a stout stick works much better. To use a knife, you must get close, and those you're fighting might have something just as nasty to hand.

I took the poker from Sally, bade her bring her candle, gathered my dressing gown about me, and led the way up into the darkened house.

Sir Lionel's house, on the north side of Portman Square, was typical of those in London at the time. We climbed the back stairs to the ground floor, emerging into a hall that ran the length of the house. A staircase with polished banisters and carved newel posts rose along one side of the hall, leading to the floors above us. Rooms opened from the opposite wall of this staircase — reception room and formal dining room on the ground floor, drawing rooms on the next floor, private chambers, including the library, above that.

I went into the dining room after checking that the front door was still bolted. The walls in there were dark wood panels hung with paintings I suspected were not very good. No expensive artwork for Sir Lionel.

The room was empty. The dining table had been cleared, a cloth cover draped over it to keep it clean between meals. The chairs were straight, the curtains drawn. Nothing to be seen.

The reception room was likewise empty, nothing disturbed, no open windows anywhere.

I was beginning to believe Sally had dreamed it all, but one never knew. A thief could have forced open a back window and be merrily burgling the house above us.

I led Sally on up the stairs. We checked the front and rear drawing rooms and found nothing amiss.

I'd check one more floor and then retire to bed. If Sir Lionel wasn't stirring, then Sally had heard John or Copley moving about for whatever their reasons.

On the next floor, I saw that the door to Sir

Lionel's library stood ajar. It was dark inside the room, no glow of a fire, lamp, or candle.

While I did not truly believe thieves would grope around in absolute darkness for valuables in Sir Lionel's library, the open door made me uneasy. I heard no sound within, not a rustle or thump of books as burglars searched for hidden caches of jewels.

I noiselessly pushed the door open and went inside.

Whatever fire had burned that day in the grate had smoldered to ashes. Sally kept bumping into the back of me, because she held the candle and stared into the flame until she was night-blind. But I could see a bit by the streetlight that glittered through the front windows, the curtains wide open.

What I saw was Sir Lionel. He was slumped forward over his desk, his head turned to the side, his mouth open, eyes staring sightlessly. My carving knife was buried to the hilt in his back.

Sally screeched and dropped the candle. I snatched the candle from the floor before a spark could catch the rug on fire, and raised the light high.

My entire body went numb, no feeling anywhere. "May God have mercy," I croaked, my throat tight and dry. "What a waste of a carver. And them so dear."

Chapter Four

I woke John in his attic chamber — Copley
heard Sally's scream and came down on his
own. I sent John for the constable but
ordered Copley to stay with the body while I
went downstairs and dressed myself.

By time I returned to the library, the
constable, a lad I'd seen walking his beat on
the square, had arrived with an older
sergeant. They'd lit up the room with every
lamp and candle they could find and stoked
the fire high. I imagined Sir Lionel's ghost
cringing at the expense.

The sergeant, a squat, fat man with one
string of hair across his bald pate and a wide,
thick-lipped mouth, turned to me.

"It's *your* knife, eh?"

Copley looked innocently at the ceiling,

but I knew he must have been filling the constable's ears with tales of my adventures with Sir Lionel.

"Of course it is mine," I snapped. "It came from the kitchens."

"'E made a grab for ye tonight, did 'e?" the sergeant asked. "And so you stuck your knife into 'im?"

I stared in astonishment. "Of course not. I've been in bed asleep these past hours. Why would I have come to the library in the middle of the night, in any case? My bedchamber is next to the kitchen, and I have no need to be above stairs at all."

The sergeant did not look impressed. "'E made a grab for you afore this, didn't 'e? And you stuck your knife to 'is throat?"

I switched my glare to Copley. He wouldn't meet my eye, but a smile hovered around his thin mouth. I said tartly, "That was weeks ago, and it was only to frighten him. I certainly would *not* have plunged my knife into a side of beef like Sir Lionel Leigh-Bradbury. It would ruin the knife. Carvers are expensive."

The constable's eyes glittered a way I didn't like. "But it was *your* knife. It would be 'andy."

"Absolute nonsense. Why would I carry my kitchen knife upstairs to the master's rooms?"

"Because 'e sent for you, and you were frightened. You brought your knife to make you feel safe-like."

"Don't be ridiculous. If I'd feared to answer his summons, I'd have stayed securely in my kitchen, or asked John to come with me. He's quite a strong lad."

The sergeant pointed a broad finger at me. "You 'ad a go at 'im before, Mr. Copley says. This time, you went too far, and did 'im."

My mouth went dry, but I kept up my bravado. "I did not kill him, you ignorant lout. Why should I?"

"Who did then? With your sticker?"

I clenched my hands. "Anyone could have taken the knife from the kitchen."

"Mr. Copley says you keep 'em put away special. No one else would know where."

"Copley does," I pointed out.

Copley sneered at me. "Bitch. She stabbed 'im. She must 'ave."

I put my closed fists on my hips. "Who says so? Did you see me, Mr. Copley?"

"Yes."

My mouth popped open. He was a liar, but Copley's look was so certain that the sergeant believed him.

"I 'eard a noise and came down," Copley said. "And there was you, a-bending over the master's body, holding the knife."

Bloody man. "Of course I looked him over

when I found him here," I said, trying not to sound desperate. "He was already dead. And *you* saw nothing at all, Mr. Copley. You only came charging in because Sally was screaming, *after* we found him."

Copley scowled. "I saw ye, I tell ye."

"You saw me discovering the knife, not plunging it in," I countered, but my blood was cold. "Ask Sally." But when I looked about for the scullery maid, I did not see her or hear her anywhere.

The sergeant was obviously on Copley's side, the young constable and John confused. All men against one woman.

"No more o' this," the sergeant said severely. "You'll promenade down to the magistrate with me, missus, and he can hear your story."

My body went colder still. If I could not convince the magistrate of my innocence, I would be thrown to the wolves — or at least, to an Old Bailey trial and a jury. A long bench of men would gaze at me disapprovingly and pronounce that cooks should not stick their carving knives into their masters. And that would be the end of me.

At twenty-nine summers, I found life sweet, and I had more to live for than just myself.

I wanted to bolt. To run, run, run, snatch

up my daughter from where I'd hidden her and flee. To the countryside—no, not far enough. The Continent, or farther, to Asia, perhaps, where I could cook for some colonial nabob who wouldn't care too much what I ran from as long as I could give him his familiar English fare.

I closed my eyes, and I prayed. I hadn't gone to church in about half a dozen years, but praying and church are two different things. I begged God to have mercy on me, and I opened my eyes again.

"Very well, then," I said, straightening my shoulders. "But no cuffs, if you please. I am a respectable woman."

I lifted my chin and marched before them out of the room, down the stairs, and straight out of the house.

***

The magistrate who examined me at Bow Street was a jovial man whose rotund body betrayed that he liked his meals and missed few. I had to stand up before him while those also awaiting examination filled the room behind me—I was a nobody, and warranted no special treatment.

Most of the people at the house had been arrested in the night for theft, drunkenness, fighting, being loud and disorderly, and for prostitution. A few well-dressed solicitors wandered the crowd, looking for clients to take to barristers, but they didn't bother approaching me. I had a bit of money put by, but I doubted I'd be able to afford an eloquent, wigged barrister to argue in my defense.

The magistrate's chair creaked as he leaned over his bench and peered at me nearsightedly. "Name?"

"Katharine Holloway, sir," I said, though it was sure to be on the paper his clerk had handed him.

"And you were the mistress of Sir Lionel Leigh-Bradbury of Portman Square?"

I gave him a look of shock. "Indeed not, sir. I was his cook."

The magistrate stared at me with unblinking, light blue eyes. "His cook? Well, madam ... you certainly cooked his goose."

The stuffy room rang with laughter.

"I did not murder him, sir," I declared over the noise.

"You claim to be innocent of this crime, do you?" the magistrate asked. "Even though the butler saw you chopping his onions?" More laughter.

"Mr. Copley saw nothing," I said indignantly. "He is a drunken fool and a liar. Besides, it was a carving knife, not a chopper."

The magistrate lost his smile. "It makes no difference whether it were for skewering or filleting. The butler saw you with your sticker, and he stands by that. Do you have any witnesses as to your character? Someone who might argue for you?"

I thought quickly. Daniel leapt to mind, but I had no way of knowing where to find him. Besides, why should he speak for me, when we were only friends in passing? This magistrate, with his obnoxious sense of humor, might accuse me of being Daniel's mistress as well.

"No, sir," I said stiffly. "My family is gone. I am on my own."

"You sound proud of that fact. No woman should be pleased she has no one to take care of her."

I raised my chin. "I take care of myself."

The magistrate studied me over his bench, and I read the assessment in his face: *No better than she ought to be.*

"You take care of yourself by giving your master supper and then stabbing him through the heart?" the magistrate demanded. "I suppose you thought him ... *well served.*"

His clerks and constables as well as many of London's unwashed, roared again. I suppose this magistrate spent all his quiet time inventing quips to bring out when the opportunity arose, for the entertainment of the court.

The magistrate gave me a wide smile, betraying that his back teeth were going rotten. "Katherine Holloway, I am binding you over for the willful murder of Sir Lionel Leigh-Bradbury of Portman Square. You will be taken to Newgate to await your trial. That will give you time to *simmer in your own sauce.*"

The room went positively riotous.

I was icy with fear but refused to bow my head. I stood there, staring at the magistrate until he signaled to his bailiff. The bailiff, a tall man with wiry hair, seized my arm and pulled me from the room.

***

The jailer who led me to a cell in Newgate had legs far longer than mine, and I had to scuttle swiftly to keep up with him.

He took me down a flight of stairs to a chilly room already filled with people. The jailer shoved me roughly inside then retreated and locked the door. I stumbled and collided with a stone wall, pins falling from my hair, the dark mass of it tumbling down. I clung to that wall, unwilling to turn and face the crowd behind me.

What on earth was I to do? Who could help me? I needed a solicitor, but as I said, I doubted I could secure even the cheapest brief to stand up for me. I might appeal to Daniel, because he'd been kind to me, but even if he would be willing to help, I had no idea how to find him or where to send him word.

Daniel might not be in London at all. He disappeared from the metropolis now and again for weeks at a time, I supposed to work other odd jobs. I could send someone to search for him or for James, but still I had no way of knowing where to start looking—except at posh houses where he *might* make deliveries—nor anyone to send.

I turned around and slid down the wall to sit with my knees against my chest. I could not remain here. It was not only my own well-being I thought of—I took care of my daughter with my wages, and what would become of her if no more money went to the family she lived with? They were kind people, but not wealthy enough to care for a child not their own. No, I had to get out.

But perhaps Daniel would hear of my arrest. He'd go to Portman Square on his usual rounds and find me gone. The newspapers, not to mention the neighbors' servants, would be full of the tale of Sir Lionel's murder.

Then again, Daniel might believe with everyone else that I'd killed Sir Lionel. He'd go about his business, thinking himself well rid of me. I'd be convicted by a jury and hanged, my feet twisting in the breeze.

Copley would come to the hanging and laugh at me.

Anger at Copley nudged away despair. If I survived this, so help me, I would exact my revenge on the man. I had only a vague idea how I'd go about doing so, but I would have plenty of time to think.

The window high in the wall darkened, and I grew hungry. My fellow inmates slumped around me, grumbling quietly among themselves. The stink of urine, sweat, and human confinement blanketed the room.

"Eat this, luv. You'll feel better."

I looked up. The woman who stood over me had snarled red hair and smelled of gin and sweat, but the look in her blue eyes was kindly. Her red satin dress was almost clean and well-mended, as though she kept it carefully, but it hung on her thin frame without stays.

Her costume made me guess her profession. Yesterday, I would have swept by such a woman, perhaps thinking on the evils of the world that drove women to lowly things—where I might be myself had I not been lucky enough to learn cookery. Today, as the woman smiled at me and held out a bit of pasty, and I wanted to embrace her as a sister.

She placed the cold pie into my hands and sat down next to me as I took a hungry bite.

The pie was soggy and laden with salt, nothing like the light-crusted savory concoctions I baked myself. But at the moment, it tasted like the finest cake.

"Me name's Anne," the woman said. "You're wrong about me, you know, luv. I'm an actress."

I studied her with renewed interest but could not remember seeing her on a stage at Drury Lane or Haymarket. However, the fact that she was an actress did not necessarily mean she was a principal—one could be buried in the chorus, quietly anonymous.

"I was unjustly accused," I said, brushing a tear from my cheek.

"Ain't we all, luv? But me old lad will come for me."

Alas, I did not have an old lad, but I did have a lass who needed to be taken care of. If perhaps I *did* get word to Daniel, I would at least ask him to see that she got the stash of money I had managed to put by. Daniel could be trusted with that, I felt certain.

But now that I had time to think, what did I know about Daniel, really? Next to nothing. He'd been a bolstering help to me these last few weeks, and he flirted with me, but in a friendly, harmless way. He never tried anything improper, though he must know by now that I might not say no to improper advances from Daniel.

I knew nothing of Daniel beyond that. Not where he dwelled or who his family was nor what he did when I did not see him. I only knew that I wanted to lean my head against his strong shoulder, feel him stoke my hair, and hear him say, "There now, Kat. Never you worry. I'll see to everything."

I chewed on the pasty and remained miserable.

***

The next morning, Anne was released. I clung to her hand when she said good-bye, knowing hers might be the last kind face I ever saw. I begged her to look for a man called Daniel McAdam and tell him what had become of me. She promised to do her best.

Anne went out, and I cried. I wept hard into my skirt and huddled like everyone else. I was thirsty, exhausted, and worried for my fate.

Later that day, the door to the common room opened, and the bailiff bellowed, "Mrs. Holloway!"

I scrambled to my feet, my heart beating wildly, my limbs cramped from sitting on the cold stone floor. I had no idea what was happening—was it time for my trial already? Or perhaps the magistrate simply wanted me back so he could make a few more jokes at my expense.

I found, to my astonishment, that the person the bailiff took me to in the jailer's room was James. Still more astonished when James said, "I'm to take you home, Mrs. Holloway. You won't stay here another minute."

I had no words, not to thank James, not to ask questions. As I stood like a mute fool, James took my hand and pulled me from the jailer's room, through the courtyard, and out the formidable gate into the light of day. Or at least a rainy afternoon.

The area around Newgate was a busy one. James had to walk me through the bustle a long way before he pushed me into a hansom cab in Ludgate Hill.

I finally found my tongue to ask questions, but James did not enter the cab with me. He only slammed the door and signaled the cabby to go. I craned my head to call out to him as the cab jerked forward, but James gave me a cheerful wave and faded into the crowd.

Had Daniel rescued me? I wondered. If so, where was he? And why wasn't James coming with me?

James had said he'd been sent to take me home. What did he mean by *home?* Sir Lionel's house would go to whoever inherited the baronetcy—a younger brother, nephew, cousin. If his heir did not want a cook who'd been arrested for murdering the previous master, then I had no home to go to.

The cab took me, however, directly to Portman Square, and Sir Lionel's house.

Chapter Five

Daniel waited for me on the stairs that led down to the scullery. He ran up them with his usual verve to assist me from the hansom, then he paid the cabby and took me down into the kitchens.

I was shaking with hunger, worry, and exhaustion. I was grimy and dirty, my clothes filthy. A long bath, a hearty meal, and a good sleep would help me considerably, but I had not the patience for any of those.

I broke from Daniel and faced him, hands on hips. "Explain yourself, Mr. McAdam."

In spite of my bravado, my voice shook, my weakened knees bent, and I swayed dangerously.

Daniel caught me and steered me to the stool where I'd sat sharpening my knives the night Sir Lionel had come down. As I caught my breath, Daniel found the kettle, filled it with water, and set it on the stove, which had already been lit.

"Nothing to explain." Daniel moved smoothly about, collecting cups and plates from the cupboards, and rummaged in the pantry for leftover seed cake and a crock of butter. He knew his way around a kitchen, that was certain. "James told me you were in trouble, and I went along to see what I could do."

"But I was released," I said, trying to understand. "No one is released from Newgate. No one like me, anyway."

"Ah, well, the magistrates were made to see that they had no reason to keep you. The fellow who examined you is a fool, and the charge of murder has been dismissed."

I stared at him in astonishment. Daniel poured water, now boiling, into a teapot. He brought the pot to the table, and when the tea had steeped a few minutes, poured out a cup and shoved it and a plate of buttered seedcake at me.

"Get that inside you. You'll feel better."

Indeed, yes. I fell upon the feast and made short work of it. Soon I was no longer hungry and thirsty, but I remained half-asleep and filthy.

"What did you do?" I asked. "I sent Anne

to find you, but I thought perhaps you'd do no more than see I had a solicitor, if that."

Daniel finished off his tea and poured himself another cup. "If you mean Anne the actress, yes, she did find James—James is a friend of her son's. But James had already seen you being arrested from here. He followed you to Bow Street and realized you were being taken off to Newgate. After that, he legged it to me and told me all. I regret you had to stay the night in that place, but I could not put things in motion sooner. I'm sorry."

I listened in amazement. "You mystify me more and more. Why should you apologize, let alone rush to my rescue? *How* did you rush to my rescue? I'm only a cook, not a duchess, with no one to speak for me."

Daniel lifted his dark brows. "Are you saying a cook should be tried and condemned for a murder she did not commit, because she is *only* a cook?"

I was too tired to argue with him, or even to understand what he was saying. "How do you know I didn't murder Sir Lionel? It was my knife in his back."

"Which someone other than you took from this kitchen and used. Someone evil enough to push the blame onto to you." Daniel sat down, comfortably pouring himself a cup of tea. He pulled a flask from his pocket, tipped a drop of whiskey into it, then a drop into mine, if you please.

He went on. "If you *had* killed Sir Lionel, why would you leave the knife in him instead of cleaning it up or getting rid of it? Why would you go happily back to bed to wait for the constables to arrive instead of running away? It was you who raised the alarm and sent for the police, wasn't it?"

"Yes." I had done all that. It seemed so long ago now.

Daniel sipped his tea, and I took another drink of mine. Whatever spirits he'd poured into the tea danced on my tongue and warmed my gullet.

Daniel watched me over his cup. "Tell me about these people who came to dinner with Sir Lionel last evening."

I could barely remember. "Mrs. Watkins would know better than I about his guests. She served at table, because Copley was a mess."

"Mrs. Watkins doesn't seem to be here. In fact, the staff have deserted the house. Does Mrs. Watkins have another address?"

I clattered my teacup to its saucer, my hands shaking. "Mrs. Watkins has a sister in Pimlico—Sally, the scullery maid, told me she'd gone there, if I remember aright. However, if you imagine I can give you the particulars of all the people who worked here and where they might be, along with the names and address of the friends who visited Sir Lionel last night ..." I broke off, no longer certain where the sentence had been taking me. "You clearly have never been up before a magistrate and thrown into a common cell at Newgate for a night. It clouds the memory."

"Oh, haven't I?" Daniel's dark eyes twinkled. "But that's a tale for another day. Come along, Kat. You have a good rest, and we'll talk when you wake."

I found myself on my feet, again supported by Daniel. "I'm wretched dirty. I need a wash."

"I have plenty of hot water going on the stove. Off we go."

He steered me to my little bedroom and then went back out to carry in steaming water and pour it into my basin. Daniel left me to it, saying a cheerful good-night.

I was so exhausted I simply stripped off every layer of clothing I wore and dumped them on the floor. I washed the best I could, then crawled into bed, still damp, in my skin.

Some believe it is very wicked to sleep without clothes, but I'd already been a sinner, and I couldn't see that God would care very much whether or not I pulled on a nightgown. I was asleep as soon as my head touched my pillow, in any case.

***

When I woke, it was bright daylight. I spent some time trying to convince myself that everything that had happened to me had been a bad dream, and that I'd rise as usual and go out into my kitchen to cook. I had an idea for tea cakes with caraway and rosemary that I wanted to try.

I threw back the covers to find myself unclothed, which reminded me of my quick bath, after which I'd been too tired to don a nightdress. This told me my adventures had been real enough—I was usually quite modest and would never risk being caught without any sort of clothing on my body.

The events of the night before notwithstanding, I rose and did my toilette, put on a clean frock and apron, pinned up my unruly hair, and set my cook's cap on my head. The familiar routine comforted me, and besides, I had no idea what else to do.

When I opened the door, the sharp smell of frying bacon came to me. I moved out to the kitchen to find Daniel at the stove, cooking. The urchin, James, a bit cleaner than he usually was, sat at the kitchen table.

When I looked at James this morning, I noticed something I had been too distracted to note in the past—he and Daniel had the same eyes. But then, I hadn't seen the two together when James's face hadn't been covered with dirt. Now I saw that the shape of James's jaw, the jut of chin, the manner in which he sat sipping a mug of tea, mirrored Daniel's almost exactly.

"You're his son," I exclaimed to James. I had no idea whether this fact was a secret, but I was too bewildered and tired to guard my tongue.

James gave me his good-natured look, and Daniel glanced over his shoulder at me. "Ah, Kat," Daniel said. "Awake at last. You slept the day away, and a night."

I rocked on my feet, disoriented. "Did I?"

"Indeed. I didn't have the heart to wake you yesterday, but I knew you'd be hungry this morning. Sit down—these eggs are almost finished."

"You have changed the subject," I said. "As usual when you don't wish to answer. Why did you not tell me James was your son? Why did *you* not tell me?" I shot at James.

James shrugged. "Embarrassing, innit? For me, I mean. T' have to admit *he* sired me?"

"I don't see why," I said. "You could do much worse than Mr. McAdam."

James grinned. "Suppose."

Daniel shot him a weary look, which made James more amused. I realized they must banter like this all the time. It reminded me of the jokes I shared with my daughter, and my heart squeezed.

By habit, I brought out my bin of flour and the sponge starter I kept on a shelf beside the icebox. I stopped after lugging the flour bin to the middle of the table. Who was I baking for? Did I still even have employment? And why were Daniel and James here, when no one else seemed to be?

"Where is everyone?" I asked. "Did Mrs. Watkins return? Copley? Sally?"

James answered, Daniel still at the stove. "The house be empty. Dangerous, that. Anyone could come in and make off with the silver."

"Have they?" I asked. "Was Sir Lionel robbed? And that's why he was killed?"

My hands measured the flour and bubbly starter into a bowl, and I took up a wooden spoon to mix it all together. The familiar feel of my muscles working as the dough grew stiffer calmed me somewhat. If there'd only be three of us today, I wouldn't need more than one loaf.

I stirred in the flour along with a dash of water and a smidgen of salt, then scraped the dough onto my table and began to knead. Neither Daniel nor James admonished me to stop. I'd refuse anyway—the vigorous kneading helped my agitation. I dumped the ball of dough into a clean bowl, covered it with a plate, and set it aside to rise.

As I wiped my floury hands, Daniel

shoved a large helping of bacon and eggs at me. "Eat all that. Then we'll talk."

"Talk." I picked up the fork he'd laid beside the plate, suddenly hungry. James, likewise, was digging into the repast. "I think I never want to talk again. Perhaps I'll retire to the country. Grow runner beans and pumpkins, and bake pies the rest of my life."

"I'd eat 'em," James said. "She's a bloody fine cook, Dad."

"Watch your language around a lady, lad." Daniel scraped back a chair, sat down, and watched us both eat. He wasn't partaking and didn't say why, but I was beyond curiosity at this point.

Once I was scraping my plate and finishing off my second cup of tea, Daniel said, "Kat, I want you to tell me about the meal you served to Sir Lionel. Every detail. Leave nothing out."

"Why?" I came alert, able to now that I had a bit more inside me.

Daniel laid his hands on the table, giving me a kindly look, but I saw something watchful behind the compassion. "Just tell me."

It was the same gaze I often found myself giving him. Wanting to trust him, but knowing so little about him I was not certain I could.

"There was nothing wrong with my

meal," I said firmly. "Was there?"

James frowned across at his father. "What are you getting at, Dad? You're upsetting her."

"Sir Lionel didn't die from the knife thrust," Daniel said, far too calm for the dire words he spoke. "That wound was inflicted post mortem. Sir Lionel had already been dead, though not for long, of arsenical poisoning. His guests, Mr. and Mrs. Fuller, also suffered from poisoning. Mr. Fuller died in the night. Mrs. Fuller, her doctor says, has a chance at recovery, but he can't say for certain whether she will live."

Chapter Six

I sat staring for a full minute, perhaps two,
my mouth hanging open. James looked no
less astonished than I did. James had helped
me with that meal, not only cleaning the fish
and fowl but laying out ingredients for me,
learning to chop mushrooms, and stirring up
dough.

"No arsenic could have been in *my*
supper," I said, when my tongue worked
again. "They must have come by the poison
elsewhere."

Daniel shook his head. "The coroner who
examined the body said that the poison had
entered the stomach at the same time as your
meal. I'm sorry, Kat. You must take me
through every dish. Please."

"Well, it could not have been in my food,

could it?" I said in rising worry. "You brought me most of the ingredients that night, and I taste everything. If arsenic had been slipped into the sauces in my kitchen, it would have killed me too. And all the staff. I always hold a portion back to serve with our supper."

"Tell me," Daniel said gently.

I heaved a sigh. I could barely remember my name let alone everything I'd made that fatal evening, but I closed my eyes in recall.

"A cream of leek soup. Whitefish with a velouté—a thickened broth and wine sauce. A salad of greens with a lime dressing and tart apples, asparagus with boiled eggs, roasted squab stuffed with peppercorns with a red wine sauce. A fricassee of mushrooms. There wasn't time for rolls with all this, so I made savory scones instead. For pudding, a thin chocolate soup to start, then custard tart with whatever berries I could find and a burnt sugar sauce. Copley chose the wine for me—perhaps *he* put poison in the wine, for whatever twisted reason he had. He's a villain; I've always said so."

Daniel shook his head. "There was nothing in the glasses, or the bottles. The coroner worked all night, testing everything he could."

"How do you know all this? Was there an inquest?"

Daniel shrugged. "He told me. He's a friend of mine."

Daniel McAdam, friends with a coroner. Why was I not surprised? "But how did he find the wine glasses?" I asked. "And the wine? Sally scrubbed everything and put it away."

"Not the wine glasses. She'd left them. The wine was still open in the butler's pantry. The police took all this away while you were ... detained."

The prison came back to me with a rush. I pinched my fingers to my nose, willing it away. When I opened my eyes, I found Daniel looking at me with such sympathy mixed with self-chastisement that it made me a bit dizzy.

I drew a breath, continuing the argument to stop the wild thoughts in my head. "The poison could *not* have been in the food," I said. "I told you, I taste everything before I allow it to go up, and every person downstairs had a helping of what every person upstairs ate. And we're all hale—well, I am, and James here appears to be."

"We're looking for the other staff," Daniel said. "We'll know soon enough."

I fixed him with a stern look. "If the coroner believes the cook poisoned the entire dinner party then why am I not still in Newgate?"

"Because of James," Daniel said, unworried. "If you had poured a box of arsenic into any of your dishes, James would have seen. You could, I suppose, have built yourself an immunity to arsenic so it wouldn't hurt you, but I know James did not. And he's not sick at all."

No, James was very healthy indeed, and listening with interest. He asked the question that was next in my mouth. "Why do you want to know all about the food, then, Dad? If you already know she didn't do it?"

Daniel opened his hands on the table. "To decide which dish might best conceal it, and how it was served. The wine and peppercorn sauce, the mushrooms, and the burned sugar on the pudding interest me most. They could have disguised the taste."

I only watched him, bewildered. "But who would have introduced this poison? I place the dishes in the lift myself. Are you saying you believe someone very small was hiding in the dumbwaiter with a vial of poison? Or something as nonsensical? Or do you believe Mrs. Watkins did it, or John, as they served the meal? Sally went nowhere near the food at all — she was busy washing up all my pots and pans."

"I can rule out none of them," Daniel said.

I blew out my breath. "I cannot imagine why on earth Mrs. Watkins, John, or Sally would do such a thing. None of them are mad, I don't think."

"They are not here either," Daniel pointed out. "Once you were taken away, John disappeared, as did your scullery maid, as well as your butler and several choice bottles of wine."

"Of course," I said in exasperation. "Copley took the wine to sell, no doubt—he refuses to drink the stuff himself. I imagine the others didn't return because they thought they had no place here anymore. Sally was terrified and fled before I was even arrested."

"Perhaps," was all Daniel would say. "Would it be too much for you, Kat, to cook the same meal, as you did that night? So I can see exactly how it was prepared?"

At the moment, I never wanted to cook anything again. But I heaved a sigh, climbed to my feet, and went through the larder to see what foodstuffs I'd need.

I had everything but the mushrooms, berries, fresh fish, and birds. James was dispatched to procure those. The leftover greens were a bit wilted, but edible, apples drying, but again, usable.

I set everything out as I remembered. A bit difficult because I never cooked to an exact recipe—I knew what went into each dish from experience, then I threw in a bit of this or that I had on hand or left out things I did not, so each meal was unique. A long time ago, when I'd first been a cook's assistant, I'd doggedly learned every step of a recipe and followed it religiously, until a famous chef I met told me to trust my own instincts. After that, my skills rose quickly.

I tried to remember what I'd done as I worked. I set Daniel to helping me chop leeks and greens, core the apples, stir the roux for the velouté, and cream the butter for the scones.

Daniel proved to be quite skilled at cookery, though it was clear he'd never handled a chef's knife before. I had to show him, with my hand over his, how to chop the leeks. His skin was warm, his breath on my cheek, warmer.

I might have stayed in the circle of his arm for a while longer had not James come banging back in. I nearly cut myself scrambling away from Daniel, who moved the knife safely aside, his eyes alight with amusement.

I set Daniel to washing and chopping the mushrooms, and James competently cleaned the fish in the scullery.

We created the meal again, which took the rest of the day, and then partook of it, enjoying the lightness of leek soup, the savory fish, the tenderness of the game birds with peppercorns, the sweet and tart tastes in the salad. The scones came out light and crumbly, the custard creamy with the bright bite of berries to finish.

When we ended the meal, Daniel pushed back his plate, clattered his fork to it, and let out a sigh. "You are an artist, Kat."

"It's only a bit of cookery," I said modestly, but I was pleased.

James wiped his mouth with the napkin I'd given him. "'Tis bloody hard work. All that, and you eat it in ten minutes."

"*You* eat it in ten minutes," Daniel said with fatherly fondness. He took a sip of the wine I'd brought out of the butler's pantry for the peppercorn sauce.

Daniel seemed to know about wine—he didn't quaff it but savored it, pronouncing the vintage excellent. He was a paradox, was Daniel, though I had long since discarded the belief that he was a simple delivery man.

"You do well in the kitchen," I told James. "You learn quickly and have a feel for the food. Perhaps you could study a bit and become a chef."

"A chef?" James snorted. "Cooking for pampered gentlemen who complain when their dinner hasn't been boiled long enough? No, thank you."

"Well." Daniel leaned back in his chair. "There was nothing wrong with that meal. Plenty of opportunities for you to slip in the poison, and you too, James—and me—but if everyone in the kitchen ate of the dishes, and you and James are well, I cannot see how the poison came from the meal as you cooked it."

"Thank you very much," I said. "You might have taken my word for it before we did all that work." Not that I'd eaten so well in a long time. I suspected part of Daniel's motive had been to partake in an expertly cooked elegant meal, which I doubted came along for him very often. I'd rather liked cooking with Daniel—and James, of course.

Daniel and James obligingly helped me clean up. I expected them, as men often did, to abandon me once the enjoyment was over, but James scrubbed plates and Daniel dried them with good cheer.

I told them to leave me after that. I had nowhere to go and would make do with my bed here tonight, but tomorrow, I'd look for other digs and a new place.

James departed, his pockets full of leftover scones. Daniel lingered on the doorstep. "Are you certain you'll be all right, Kat?"

"Not entirely." The kitchen was echoing without Daniel and James in it, the rooms above me, too silent. However, the street was busy and noisy, and the neighbors and their servants were near to hand. "I don't have much choice do I? But I am made of strong stuff, do not worry."

"Hmm." Daniel glanced at the ceiling, as though he could see the entire house above us. "Lock this door behind me then. I've already bolted the front door but keep the door at the top of the back stairs locked. And don't go out until morning."

His caution unnerved me. I felt the weight of the house above us, empty and waiting. I drew a breath and repeated that I'd be all right, and at last, Daniel departed.

I locked the kitchen door then scurried up the back stairs to the door at the top, its green baize tight and unblemished, as though nothing untoward had occurred beyond it. I opened the door and peered out into the cold darkness of the house.

I was too sensible to believe in spirits, but the shadows seemed to press at me. Sir Lionel had died here, alone and unpitied.

I quickly closed that door, locked it, and descended again to the kitchen, where I rechecked the back door and made certain none of the high windows were open. The kitchen was stuffy with the windows closed, but I'd put up with it.

I retired to bed, but I could not sleep for a good long time, as tired as I was. I kept picturing the rooms upstairs, dark, deserted, silent.

At last I did drift off, only to be woken by

a loud   *thump*. Then came a creak of floorboard above me. Someone was in the house.

I had a moment of panic, wanting to put the bedcovers over my head and pretend it hadn't happened. But I hardened my resolve and sat up.

Burglars must have broken in—empty houses were good targets, especially those belonging to rich men. Sir Lionel's heir would no doubt arrive to take possession soon, but until then, a house full of silver, wine, and other valuables was a sitting duck waiting to be plucked.

I wasn't having it. I sprang quietly out of bed, pulled on a blouse and skirt over my nightclothes and found my good, stout boots. I'd run for the constable who patrolled the street—never mind he'd had a hand in my arrest—and bring him in to the take the thieves.

As I left my tiny bedchamber and made my way through the short hall to the kitchen, I heard the burglar start down the back stairs.

Damn and blast. The entire expanse of the kitchen lay between me and the back door. I knew why they'd come down here—the master's collection of wine and much of the silver lay in the butler's pantry beyond the kitchen.

I'd have to risk it. Taking a deep breath, I scurried across the flagstone floor toward the scullery and the back door.

A dark figure leapt down the last part of the stairs and grabbed me before I could reach for the door latch—the door was already unlocked, I saw belatedly. I let out a scream. A hand clamped over my mouth and dragged me back into the kitchen. I fought like mad, kicking and flailing with my fists.

"For God's sake, Kat, *stop*!"

Daniel's voice was a hiss in my ear, and a second later, I realized it was he who held me. I broke away. "What the devil are you doing, frightening me out of my wits?" I asked in a fierce whisper.

"Shh." He put a finger to my lips.

I understood. Though it had been Daniel creeping down to the kitchen, someone was still upstairs, robbing the place.

"It's Copley," Daniel said into my ear.

I started in indignation. "That rat. We should run for the constable. Catch him at it."

"The police are already waiting outside. When he runs out with the goods, they'll nab him. He won't have any excuse or chance to hide."

I went quiet as the floorboards creaked again. I might have known. "What if he comes down here?" I asked.

"Then I'll lay him out and deliver him to the Peelers."

I liked the idea, but I had to wonder. "Why are you hand in glove with the police?"

Daniel's vague shrug was maddening, but I fell silent. We traced Copley's path across the ground floor above us until he disappeared into the rear of the house.

"The garden door," Daniel said in a low voice, no more whispering. "That's how he came in. He'll find plenty of the Old Bill waiting for him as he goes out."

The nearness of Daniel was warming. "How did you know he was here at all?"

"I was watching the house, saw him pass a few times. Then he nipped around the corner to the mews behind it. I told the constable to bring some stout fellows, and I followed Copley inside."

"You were watching the house?" I was befuddled from being jerked from a sound sleep and having Daniel so close to me.

Daniel gave me a nod. "I wanted to make sure all was well. I worry about you, Kat."

He looked at me for a long moment, the touched my chin with his forefinger, leaned down, and brushed a kiss across my lips.

I was too astonished to do anything but let him. Daniel straightened, gave me a wry smile, and moved around me to let himself out the kitchen door.

A blast of cold air poured over me, but my body was warm where he'd held me. I touched my fingertips to my lips, still feeling the pressure of his soft kiss.

Chapter Seven

Daniel returned in the morning, knocking on the kitchen door, which I'd re-locked.

He'd brought James with him again, to help me with the morning chores necessary to any house, no matter I was its only resident. James whipped around, carrying in coal and helping stir up the fire, while I mixed up dough for flat muffins and fried the last of the bacon.

I kept glancing sideways at Daniel as we ate at the table, though he did not seem to notice. He said nothing about the adventure of the night before—not to mention the kiss—as if none of it were of any moment.

I was no stranger to the relations between men and women—I had a daughter, after all—but what I'd had with my husband had been sometimes painful and always far from affectionate. The gentle heat of Daniel's mouth had opened possibilities to me, thoughts I'd never explored. I'd had no idea a man could be so tender.

Daniel seemed to have forgotten all about the kiss, however. That stung, but I made myself feel better by pretending he was being discreet in front of his son.

After breakfast, I mentioned I needed to tidy myself and return to the agency to find another post, but Daniel forestalled me. "First we are visiting Mrs. Fuller."

I blinked as I set the plates on the draining board. "The woman who shared the fatal meal? She has recovered?"

"She has, and was lucky to. The coroner tells me there was a large quantity of poison in the two men, enough to kill a person several times over. Mrs. Fuller is rather stout, so perhaps the arsenic did not penetrate her system as thoroughly. Her doctors purged her well."

"Poor thing," I said. "Do you think Copley somehow added the poison to the meal? To clear Sir Lionel out of the way so he might help himself to the goods?" I contemplated this a moment, rinsing plates under the taps. "Perhaps he only pretended to be too drunk to serve that night, so the food wouldn't be connected with him."

Daniel shook his head. "I think Copley is more an opportunist than a schemer. Though he might have seen an opportunity to administer the poison and took it."

"I still don't see how. Copley is limber and thin, but I can't imagine him crouching in the dumbwaiter shaft with a bottle of poison."

Daniel gave me his warm laugh. "Nor can I. Ready yourself, and we'll go."

James finished the washing up so I could change. I put on my second-best dress, the one I kept clean for visiting agencies or my acquaintances on my day out, or my occasional jaunt to the theatre. For church and visiting my daughter, I always wore my best dress.

This gown was a modest dark brown, with black piping on cuffs, bodice, and neckline. I flattered myself that it went with my glossy brown hair and dark blue eyes. The hat that matched it—coffee-brown straw with a subdued collection of feathers and a black ribbon—set it off to perfection.

Daniel gave me a glance of approval when I emerged, which warmed me. Ridiculous. I was behaving like a smitten girl.

But then, he'd never seen me in anything but my gray work dress and apron. James grinned at me, told me I was lovely, and offered me his arm. Sweet boy.

Mrs. Fuller lived on Wilton Crescent, near

Belgrave Square. A fine address, and the mansion that went with it took my breath away. Daniel and I were let in by a side door, though James remained outside with the hired coach.

The ceilings of the house above stairs were enormously high, the back and front parlors divided by pointed arches. Plants were everywhere—we had stepped into a tropical rainforest it seemed. Rubber trees, elephant's ears, potted palms, and other exotic species I couldn't identify filled the rooms. The furniture surrounding these plants was elegantly carved, heavy, and upholstered in velvet.

The butler led us through the front and back parlors and into a bedchamber that looked out to the gardens in back of the house.

This room was as elegant as the others, the ceiling crisscrossed with beams carved like those in an Indian mogul's palace. Mosaics covered blank spaces in the ceiling, and outside in the garden, a fountain containing tiles with more mosaics burbled.

Mrs. Fuller lay on a thick mattress in an enormous mahogany bedstead with curved sides. Mrs. Fuller was indeed stout, about twice my girth, and I am not a thin woman. Her face, however, was pretty in a girlish way, the hair under her cap brown without a touch of gray.

I curtsied when the butler announced us, and Daniel made a polite bow. "I apologize for disturbing you, madam," Daniel began. "The police inspector thought Mrs. Holloway might be of assistance, as he discussed with you."

"Yes, indeed." Mrs. Fuller lifted a damp handkerchief from the bedcovers and wiped her red-rimmed eyes. "I am anxious to find out what happened. Forgive me, my dear, if I am not myself. It is still incredible to me that my dear husband is gone, and yet, here I am. You are the cook?"

"Indeed." I gave her another polite curtsy. "My condolences, ma'am. Yes, I cooked the meal, but I promise you, I never would have dreamed of tainting it in any way."

Mrs. Fuller dabbed her eyes again. "They told me you were innocent of the crime. I suppose you are suffering from this in your own way as well. Your reputation ... you are an excellent cook, my dear. If it is any consolation, I so enjoyed the meal." Her smile was weary, that of a woman trying to make sense of a bizarre circumstance.

Daniel broke in, his voice quiet. "I've asked Mrs. Holloway about what she served and how she prepared it. It would help if you described the meal in your own words, Mrs. Fuller, and tell us if any dishes tasted odd."

Mrs. Fuller looked thoughtful. I pitied her, ill and abruptly widowed. She could have doctored the food herself to kill her rich husband, of course, but her husband dying did not mean she inherited all the money. That would go to her oldest son, if she had sons, or to nephews or other male kin if she did not. She'd receive only what was apportioned to her in the will or in the marriage agreement, though the heir could be generous and give her an allowance and place to live. However, the heir did not have to, not legally.

One reason not to marry in haste was that a widowed woman might find herself destitute. Careful planning was best, as were contracts signed by solicitors, as I'd learned to my regret.

"Let me see," Mrs. Fuller began. She then listed all the dishes I had prepared, forgetting about the mushrooms at first, but she said, "oh, yes," and came back to them. No, all tasted as they should, Mrs. Fuller thought, and she heaped more praise on my cooking.

"The custard at the end was very nice," she finished, sounding tired. "With the berries, all sweetened with sugar."

She had described what I did. Nothing added or missing. She and Sir Lionel had taken coffee, while her husband had been served tea, so if the poison had been in the coffee, she would have still have been ill but her husband alive.

Daniel seemed neither disappointed nor enlightened at the end of this interview. He thanked Mrs. Fuller, who looked tired, and we began to take our leave.

As her maid ushered us out of the bedchamber, a thought struck me. "A moment," I said, turning back to Mrs. Fuller. "You said the custard and berries were sweet with sugar. I put a burnt sugar sauce on the custard, yes, but did not sprinkle more sugar on top. Is that what you meant?"

Mrs. Fuller frowned. "I meant that there was sugar in a caster that came with the tarts on the tray. We all made use of it."

"Ah," I said.

Mrs. Fuller drooped against her pillows, the handkerchief coming up to her eyes again. The maid gave us a severe look, protective of her mistress, and Daniel led me firmly from the room.

I tried to walk decorously out of the house, but I moved faster and faster until I was nearly running as we reached the carriage.

"What the devil is it, Kat?" Daniel asked as he helped me in and climbed up beside me. "What did she say that's got you agitated?"

"The caster." I beamed as James slammed the door. "*There* is your incongruity."

Daniel only peered at me. "Why?"

"Because, my dear Daniel, I never sprinkle extra sugar on my custards, especially with the berries. Ruins the contrast—the custard is plenty sweet with the burnt sugar sauce, and the slight tartness of the berries sets it off perfectly. Extra sugar only drowns the flavor. I would never have sent up a caster full of it on a tray to ruin my dessert. I didn't, in fact. That means the poison must have been in the sugar."

Daniel's eyes lit, a wonderful sight in a handsome man. "I see. The murk begins to clear."

"Does it?" I deflated a bit. "Now all we need to know is where the caster came from, who put the poison into it, and how it got on the table that night."

Daniel gave me a wise nod. "I'm sure you'll discover that soon enough."

"Don't tease. I am not a policeman, Mr. McAdam."

"I know, but perhaps you ought to be." His amusement evaporated. "I must ask the inspector how he and his men missed a container full of poison when they searched the house."

He had a point. "The poisoner obviously took it away before the police arrived," I said.

"Oh, yes, of course. Why didn't I think of that?"

The wretch. My gaze dropped to his smiling mouth, and the memory of his brief kiss stole over me. If Daniel noticed my sudden flush, he said nothing, and we arrived at Sir Lionel's house again.

Nothing for it, but we began to search the place, top to bottom, for the sugar caster. I had to first explain to James what one was.

"A small carved silver jug-like shape, with a top," I said. "Like a salt shaker, but wider and fatter."

James nodded, understanding, but try as we might, we could not find it. We searched through the dining room, opening all the doors in the sideboard and the breakfront, then I led them downstairs to the butler's pantry.

The walls were lined with shelves that housed much of Sir Lionel's collection of silver, some of it handed down for generations through the Leigh-Bradbury family. Silver kept its value where coins, stocks, banknotes, and even paintings might become worthless. Heavy silver could at least be sold for its metal content if nothing else. Sir Lionel's plate had the hallmark of a silversmith from two centuries ago and was probably worth a fortune.

I discovered that at least a third of this valuable silver was missing.

"Copley," I said, hands on hips.

Daniel, next to me, agreed. "Meanwhile— no sugar caster?"

"If it's in this house, it wasn't put back into its usual place. Did Copley rush out of here with it in his bag of stolen silver?"

"Very possibly," Daniel said. "I will question the inspector who arrested him."

I became lost in thought. How likely was it that the poisoner had tamely returned the caster to the butler's pantry, ready for Copley to steal it? Unless Copley had poisoned Sir Lionel for the express purpose of making off with the silver. Why, then, had Copley waited until Sir Lionel had been found? Why not put the things into a bag and be far away when I'd stumbled across the body? The answer was that Copley most likely hadn't known that Sir Lionel would be killed. He was an opportunist, as Daniel said.

Daniel's shoulder next to mine was warm. I did not know what to make of him. Would I ever know who he truly was?

Well, I would not let him kiss me again and then disappear, leaving me in the dark. I was a grown woman, no longer the young fool I was to let a handsome man turn my head.

I voiced the thought that we should look

for the caster in *un*usual places, and we went back to the dining room. After a long search, I spotted the sugar caster tucked into a pot containing a rubber tree plant.

The plant and its large pot stood just outside the dining room door, a nuisance I'd thought it, with its fat leaves slapping me across the back if I didn't enter the doorway straight on. As I impatiently pushed the leaves aside, I spied a glint of silver among the black earth.

I called to Daniel, and put a hand in to fish it out. He forestalled me, shook out a handkerchief, and carefully lifted it.

He carried the caster into the dining room, both of us breathless, as though the thing would explode. James fetched a napkin from the sideboard, and Daniel set the caster into the middle of it. With the handkerchief, he delicately unscrewed the top, then dumped the contents of the caster onto another napkin.

It looked like sugar—fine white sugar used to put a final taste on pastries, berries, cakes.

James put out a finger to touch the crystals, but Daniel snapped, "No!"

James curled his finger back, unoffended. "What is it?" he asked.

"Who knows?" Daniel said. "Arsenic, perhaps? Or some other foul chemical. I'm not a scientist or doctor."

"Or chemist," I said. "They sell poisons."

"True." Daniel wrapped the caster's contents in one napkin, the caster in the other, and put them all into the bag he carried.

"What will you do with those?" I asked.

"Take them to a chemist I know. Very clever, Mrs. Holloway."

"Common sense, I would have thought."

The teasing glint entered Daniel's eyes again. "Well, I have a distinct lack of common sense when I'm near you, Kat."

James rolled his eyes, and I frowned at Daniel—I refused to let him beguile me. "Be off with you, Mr. McAdam. I must put my things in order and find a place to stay. Another night in this house would not be good for my health, I think."

"I agree." Daniel gave me an unreadable look. "Where will you go?"

I had no idea. "I suppose I'll look for a boardinghouse that will take a cook whose master died after eating one of her meals. I'm certain I'll be welcomed with open arms."

Daniel didn't smile. "Go nowhere without sending me word, agreed?"

"Send word to where?" I looked him straight in the eye. "Your address, sir?"

Daniel returned my look, unblinking. "Leave a note here. I'll find it."

We continued our duel with gazes until finally Daniel gave me the ghost of a smile and turned away.

When James started to follow Daniel downstairs, I stopped him. "Where *does* he live, James?" I asked in a low voice.

James stuck his hands in his pockets. "Tell ya the truth, missus, I don't know. He finds me. He always seems to know where I am."

"And your mum?"

James shrugged, hands still in his pockets. "Never knew her. I was raised by a lady who chars for houses until he found me. But I've never stayed with him. I board with some people—respectable. He pays for it."

I was more mystified than ever. James behaved as though this were the normal course of things, though I saw a tiny flicker of hurt in his eyes that his father didn't want him rooming with him for whatever his reasons.

Daniel had banged out the front door. James rushed to catch up with him, and I closed and bolted the door behind them.

The house became eerier once they'd gone. I hastened down to my rooms, packed my things in my box, then left the box and went out again in hat and coat. I dutifully left a note for Daniel about where I was going on the kitchen table, which I'd cleaned and scrubbed after this morning's meal.

The first person I looked up was Mrs. Watkins, the housekeeper. She might have heard of a house looking for a cook, or might know where I could rest my head tonight.

Mrs. Watkins's sister lived in Pimlico. I found out exactly where by letting myself into the housekeeper's room and going through her small writing desk. Mrs. Watkins would have left all the paperwork and keys for the house for the next housekeeper, even if she'd gone in haste. I discovered everything neatly organized, as I'd thought I would.

I took an omnibus to Pimlico and found the house, a respectable address in an area of middle-class Londoners. Mrs. Watkins's sister, it turned out, ran a boardinghouse herself—for genteel, unmarried women, and Mrs. Watkins had just taken the last room.

"Mrs. Holloway!" Mrs. Watkins exclaimed in surprise when she entered the parlor to find me there. I'd asked the maid to send up word that Mrs. Watkins had a visitor, but I had not given my name.

"Good evening, Mrs. Watkins," I said.

"I heard ... I thought ..." She opened and closed her mouth, at a loss for words.

"Yes, I was taken before a magistrate, but then released." I made a dismissive gesture, as though I survived ordeals like being locked in Newgate every day.

Mrs. Watkins remained standing with hands clenched as she adjusted to this turn of events. "Well, I have to say I never thought you could have done such a thing. You have a temper on you, Mrs. Holloway, but plunging a knife into a man takes a cruelty I don't think you possess."

"The knife didn't kill him," I said. "He was poisoned. As were the others at the table. Now then, Mrs. Watkins, why did you set a sugar caster on the table when I didn't send it up with the meal?"

Mrs. Watkins gave me a perplexed frown. "What sugar caster?"

"The one Sir Lionel and his guests used to liberally sprinkle sugar all over my tart. Which they should not have—the flavor was just fine. If they'd known anything about food, those two men would be alive today."

Mrs. Watkins continued to blink at me. "You are making no sense. There was no sugar caster on the table."

"Then why did Mrs. Fuller say there was?"

"Gracious, I have no idea."

We eyed each other, two respectable-looking women standing in the middle of a carpet in a sitting room, the carved furniture and draped tables hemming us in. A lamp, already lit against gathering gloom, hissed as its wick drew up more kerosene.

The two of us were dressed similarly, our bodices tightly buttoned to our chins. I wore a jacket of dark gray wool, while Mrs. Watkins was dressed in a simple ensemble for an evening indoors. She was tall and bony, I plump and shorter of stature.

No one could have mistaken us for anything but two ladies who'd had to grub for our living, except that we had a bit more responsibility and wisdom, and had left behind the lower levels of the serving class.

And yet, was that all we were—respectable women in the upper echelon of the servant class? Who really knew anything about us? I had a daughter but no sign of a husband. Mrs. Watkins—what had she been in life? Behind the layers we showed the world, what secrets did we keep?

"Are you certain there was no sugar caster?" I asked after a silence.

"Positive."

There it was. Either Mrs. Watkins lied, or Mrs. Fuller did. Was the liar the poisoner? Or did each of them lie for some reason I could not comprehend?

I needed an independent party to tip the balance. John the footman, Sally, or even Copley. John certainly would have seen what had happened at the table that night. He wasn't the brightest of lads, but he was worth speaking to—unless he'd done the poisoning, of course. And then there was Sally. She'd discovered Sir Lionel. Her fright and shock had seemed real enough, but I had been too stunned myself to pay much attention.

I thanked Mrs. Watkins, wished her the best, and left the house, pondering over what she'd told me. If she lied about not placing or seeing the caster on the table, why had she? I had no idea. What a muddle.

John proved to be elusive. According to Mrs. Watkins's notes, which I read back at Sir Lionel's house, he'd been a cousin of Sir Lionel's coachman, but that coachman had been dismissed before I'd been employed there. The coachman now drove for a banker with a house in Dorset. John had no other relation, it seemed, and I had no idea how to go about looking for him. John might even now be in Dorset in search of a new position. Sally had a family in Southwark, the notes said, and I wondered if she'd retreated there.

I wrote a brief letter to the coachman who was John's cousin, addressed it in care of the banker in Dorset, and took it out to post.

Night had fallen. Streetlamps outside Sir Lionel's had been lit, and Portman Square teemed with people. London never really slept.

It was too late for the errand I truly wanted to run, so I began a brisk walk to a boardinghouse I'd lodged in before. Not the best, and the cook was deplorable, but needs must.

I had reached Oxford Street when I saw him.

Traffic blocked me from crossing, so I turned aside to buy a bun from a vendor. A little way behind me, a few well-dressed ladies and gentlemen were coming out of a large house and ascending into a coach.

One of the gentlemen was Daniel.

Chapter Eight

I was so astonished, I froze, the warm bun halfway to my lips.

Gone was the rather shabbily dressed man with heavy gloves and mud-splotched boots who argued in a good-natured way with his son. This gentleman wore a dark, well-tailored suit, which was clean and whole — in fact, it looked costly.

Creased trousers covered shining boots, and his overcoat against the evening chill fit him perfectly, made for him. A neatly tied cravat and a gold watch chain in his waistcoat completed the gentleman's ensemble.

Daniel's hair, instead of being its usual unruly mop, was slicked to flow behind his ears. He paused on the doorstep to set a tall silk hat on his head.

This couldn't be Daniel McAdam, could it? *My* Daniel?

My first inclination was to dart forward and look this person in the face. And if it were Daniel, ask him what the devil he meant by it.

I almost did. I hastily checked my steps, however, when I saw a woman emerge from the house and take his arm.

She was obviously a highborn lady. Her gown spoke of elegance and refinement, silk and lace, with a glitter of diamonds at her throat. Not a courtesan, I thought. While courtesans could dress as finely as any lady, this gown was demure while also being highly fashionable.

A sister, I reassured myself quickly. Or a cousin. Something innocent. But the way Daniel handed the woman into the coach told me differently. He held her hand longer than was polite, helped her inside with a touch on her waist that lingered.

A sister might laugh at his care. This lady turned and gave Daniel such a warm smile that I nearly dropped my hunk of bread.

Daniel glanced around him, scanning the street in a surreptitious manner, as I'd often seen him do — assessing the lay of the land.

That glance clinched the matter. He was Daniel, and not simply a man who resembled him. His clothes were different, but his mannerisms, the look, the way he moved — Daniel.

As his gaze roved the street, I ducked back from the streetlight, earning me a growl from a passerby I nearly trod on. I begged his pardon and pushed myself into the shadows of a house, where the gaslight didn't reach.

I could scarcely breathe. Daniel finished scrutinizing the street and climbed up into the coach with the lady. The other lady and gentleman who'd come out of the house had entered the carriage as I'd watched Daniel. A footman from the house shut the door and signaled the coachman to go.

My heart was like stone as the carriage creaked away. I handed the uneaten bun to a beggar, drew my jacket about me, and walked on.

***

The landlady at my old boardinghouse let me have a small room at the top of the house. It was cramped and cold, and I grew nostalgic for my cubbyhole behind the kitchen fireplace at Sir Lionel's.

It was not only the cold that kept me awake. I saw Daniel over and over in my mind, setting his fashionable hat on his head and touching the lady's back as he handed her into the carriage.

He'd been comfortable in those clothes, as

comfortable as he was in his rough trousers and worn knee boots. He knew how to wear a gentleman's suit without awkwardness, and the lady with him seemed to find nothing amiss

Which was the real Daniel?

Or had I been mistaken? Daylight had been waning, gas lamps throwing a harsh glare on the street. Perhaps I had spied a man who had greatly resembled Daniel … down to the turn of his head, the flick of his eyes, his way of looking about as though memorizing everything in sight.

The logical way to resolve the issue was to return to the house at Oxford Street, knock on the door, and demand to know if Daniel had been there last night. I had a good excuse to go to the house—I was a cook looking for a new position. Cooks didn't generally walk the streets knocking on doors, but it could happen. I would ask the domestics there about the household, perhaps make friends with their current cook, and discover what was what.

Another logical course was to ask Daniel point blank. That is, if I ever saw the man again and could strike up the courage to question him. I might not like the answers.

Or I could forget about Daniel altogether, visit my agency, find another place, and resolve to speak to him no more.

None of the scenarios satisfied me. I rose in the morning, cross and sandy-eyed, nibbled at the breakfast of undercooked bacon, overdone eggs, half-burned toast, and ice-hard butter, and went out. I wended my way back to Portman Square and Sir Lionel's, where all was quiet, to fetch my box.

I made certain that the kitchen and my room had been put to rights—when Sir Lionel's heir took possession of the house I didn't want him blaming the previous staff for anything untoward. I'd need help shoving my trunk up the stairs outside, so I put on my hat with the feathers and black ribbon, and went out to ask the neighbor's boot boy to assist me.

I found James sitting on the scullery stairs. "Morning, Mrs. Holloway," he sang out.

I jumped. "James," I said, hand on my heart. "Good heavens, you should not do that."

"Sorry, missus."

I felt awkward speaking to him now. Did James know? Were James and his father deceiving me together, or did Daniel keep his own son in the dark as to whoever he truly was?

"No matter," I said. "You're just the lad. Can you help me with my box? I have a cart on the way …"

A cart pulled up in the street at that

moment, and Daniel climbed down from it, his feet in scuffed boots landing outside the railings above me. I gulped and hastened back into the kitchen, not ready to encounter him just yet.

Daniel came ruthlessly inside. James darted past him to begin shoving my large, square trunk across the flagstones, but Daniel stood in the middle of the kitchen, his soft cap crumpled in his hand. His hair was its usual rumpled mess, his boots muddy, his loose neck cloth letting me glimpse a sliver of chest.

This was Daniel McAdam. The worker, unashamed of doing manual labor for a living. I had to have been mistaken about the other.

Daniel's good-natured expression was in place, as though he'd spent the night doing nothing more than drinking ale with his fellow delivery men in a public house.

"I thought you'd be agog to know what I learned from my chemist," he was saying.

I'd forgotten about the blasted chemist, and I *was* curious, drat him. "Did he discover what was in the sugar caster?"

"He did," Daniel said readily. "Nothing but sugar."

"Oh." I blinked, my thoughts rearranging themselves. "Then what was it doing in the plant pot? And why did Mrs. Watkins swear up and down that the caster hadn't been on the table at all?"

Daniel's gaze sharpened. "Mrs. Watkins, the housekeeper? When did she say this?"

"Yesterday afternoon, when I went to call on her. She's staying with her sister, Mrs. Herbert, who runs a boardinghouse. I believe I told you about the sister in Pimlico."

"And you went there to confront her alone?" Daniel's look was narrow and so angry that I blinked. "Without a word to me?"

"I left you a note." I pointed to the table, where the note had lain, though I'd put it on the fire this morning, no longer needed.

"You should not have gone alone," Daniel said sternly, his tone unforgiving. "You should have told me and had me come with you."

"To a ladies' boardinghouse?" I asked, my eyes widening. "They wouldn't have let you in. Besides, you had business of your own last night, did you not?"

Was it my imagination, or did he start? "I could have put any business off. This is important."

I had been avoiding looking straight at him, but now I lifted my chin and met his gaze.

"What *was* your business last evening?" I asked. "Did it take you to Oxford Street?"

Daniel focused hard on me as he went more still than I thought a human being could become. Everything affable about him fell away, and I was left looking at a man I did not know.

James and the neighbor's boot boy were pushing my box up the outside stairs— *thump, bump*—bantering with each other, laughing. Inside the kitchen, all was silence.

Daniel studied me with a gaze I could not read. No more warmth and helpful friendliness in his eyes, no more clever delivery man trying to find out who'd killed Sir Lionel. He was not even the cool gentleman I'd spied last night in Oxford Street. Daniel stood upright like a blade and looked as deadly.

"Then I *did* see you," I said softly.

His one, short nod lanced my heart. A rich gentleman did not pretend to be a poor one without ulterior reason—nor the other way around. Not very good reasons, either.

"The lady," I said, wanting to know the worst. "She is your wife?"

A shake of the head, as perfunctory as the nod. "No."

"Affianced?"

Daniel waited a bit before the next shake of head.

"Lover? I must admit, Mr. McAdam, I am quite curious."

"I know you are." His words were quiet, as were his eyes. "Mrs. Holloway, I have done you a great disservice."

He hadn't answered my last question. The knife in my heart twisted. "How so?" I asked. "By lying about who you truly are? I have known others who have done the same thing." The father of my daughter, for instance.

"I know."

It took a moment for me to comprehend those two simple words. *I know.* My beloved hat felt too tight on my head.

"What on earth do you mean by that?" I snapped. "You know what?"

Daniel's expression didn't change. "I know that the man who married you already had a living wife. That he abandoned you and left you to face the world alone, with a child. That you fought hard to gain the position you have. That you're a bloody good cook." The corners of his lips twitched as he said this last, but I'd never warm to his smile again.

"And yet," I said. "I know nothing about you."

"That is something I cannot remedy. Not yet. I regret that, Mrs. Holloway, believe me."

I noted that he no longer addressed me as *Kat*. "Well, I *don't* believe you. I was a fool ever to believe in you." I stopped the tears in my voice and cleared my throat. "Thank you for releasing me from prison, Mr. McAdam — or whatever your name is. Now, I must get on. I have to find another place so I may earn my keep, and my daughter's. Good day to you."

"I have already found another place for you."

I stopped in the act of pulling on a glove. "I beg your pardon?"

Daniel took a step toward me, cool and efficient. "The Earl of Clarendon, in Berkeley Square, needs a cook, one with excellent skills. You may start there anytime you wish."

Anger boiled through me, stronger than I'd felt in a very long time. How dare he? Daniel had caused me to make an idiot of myself, and now he sought to repair the damage by sending me off to the home of ... who? One of his dear friends? His relations?

"No, thank you," I said coldly. "I will go to my agency and see what is on their books. As is proper. Good *day*, Mr. McAdam."

"Kat, you need to take the position," Daniel said, his voice unyielding. "That and no other."

I thunked my small handbag onto the table. "Why? You tell me right now, Daniel. Why should I believe a word you say?"

His eyes flickered. "Because you will be safe there."

"*Safe?* From whom?"

"From those who wish you harm because of me." Every word was as hard as stones. "Sir Lionel died because of me. I did not kill him, but I caused his death. That is why I knew you never killed him—stabbed, poisoned, or otherwise, no matter what he'd done. When I learned he'd made advances to you, I warned him off and ensured that James or I watched you at all times. That is another reason I know you did not kill him— James or I would have seen."

I struggled for breath. "What are you talking about? *You* warned him off? What have you to do with Sir Lionel Leigh-Blasted-Bradbury?"

"Kat, believe me, I wish I could unburden myself to you, but I cannot. Not because I do not trust you, but because it wouldn't be safe for you. Or your daughter. Suffice it to say Sir Lionel mixed with people he should not have. In exchange for him continuing to live a free man, he was to tell me of all interactions he had with these people and the information they imparted to him. I believe that somehow, they got wind of what he was doing, and killed him."

"By poisoning my dinner?"

"By poisoning him *somehow*. I thought

Mrs. Fuller had done so, making herself sick as a blind. But she was genuinely distressed and confused and grieving for her husband. I don't believe now she knew what dealings her husband had. The sugar caster ... I admit I have no idea how that fits in."

"I see." I said the words, but I saw nothing. I only knew that I had been made to think one way, when events had been something else entirely.

I could blame Daniel for deceiving me, but I mostly blamed myself. I'd been flattered by his attentions and preened myself because the handsome Daniel had interest in me.

"I thank you for explaining," I said, finishing drawing on my gloves. "I shall be boarding at Handley House in King Street, Covent Garden, if I can help you further in the matter of Sir Lionel. Good morning."

Daniel stepped in front of me. "I wish you to take the post in Berkeley Square."

His tone was firm, but I was tired of being told what to do. "No, thank you," I said. "I will find another position soon. I will send you word—somehow—of where if it will make you feel better."

I marched around him, straightening my hat as I went, and this time Daniel did not try to prevent me.

I went up the stairs without looking back, and to the street. I told James where I needed the trunk to be sent, and made my way to catch a hansom cab to take me to my boardinghouse.

After settling myself in there, I paid a visit to my daughter.

Chapter Nine

Once my so-called husband had vanished into the mists, and it became clear that I had never been legally married, I knew I'd have to work hard or my child would starve. Because I was unlikely to find a post as a disgraced woman with an illegitimate offspring in tow, I called myself by my maiden name—appending "Mrs." to it—and found a family who would foster my daughter.

The woman who took her in had been a friend to me since childhood. She'd been a kindly girl and was now a kindly woman. Her husband was good-natured and liked children, so my Grace lived with them and their four offspring in their tiny house and seemed to be happy.

Grace was never formal with me and unashamedly ran to throw her arms around me when I arrived. At ten years old, she was a beauty and possessed an understanding beyond her years. Grace did not resent the fact that I could not have her living with me where I cooked. She understood that we had to make our way in the world the best we could. One day, she said, she'd do the work and look after *me*.

I took her to walk with me in Hyde Park— our treat, after ices from a vendor. "Is everything all right, Mama?" she asked, slipping her hand in mine. Grace was always able to sense my moods.

I had not told my daughter about the horror of being arrested and imprisoned. I'd told my friend who looked after Grace but she'd agreed it wise not to mention it to the children, bless her.

"I am sad and confused, Grace," I said. "That is all."

"Because of the murder in Sir Lionel's house?"

So, she at least knew about that. Well, it is difficult to keep sensational news from a child, no matter how sheltered.

I admitted as much. "I will have to find another place. I'm not sure where it will be."

"I know *you* didn't poison anyone with your cooking, Mama," Grace said. "It must have been someone else."

"Yes, indeed. The puzzling thing is how." I pondered, forgetting to be cautious. "The arsenic was in no dish of mine. Mrs. Fuller said there was sugar; Mrs. Watkins says there was none. The sugar in the caster was tested — it was only sugar."

"Perhaps the caster was replaced with another," Grace said. "Afterward."

"An intriguing idea." I tapped my lower lip. "But why put the one with only sugar in the plant pot?"

"They meant to retrieve it later?" Grace, with her pointed face and fine hair, looked nothing more than a sweet-tempered child, but I knew what a quick mind her young face hid. "They meant to switch it for the clean one, but were interrupted. They didn't have time to fetch it out of the plant."

"Hm. A line I will have to investigate, I think."

"Will you tell me? If I'm right, will you tell me what happens?"

I squeezed her hand. "Of course I will."

We walked back to the omnibus and returned to my friend's home. My visit to Grace had lightened my heart. I never mentioned Daniel during this visit, and as I left my daughter, I realized he didn't matter. As long as I had Grace in my life, the attentions of deceitful gentlemen were of no moment to me.

I could not keep my thoughts entirely from Daniel, unfortunately, try as I might. As I made my way back to the boardinghouse, I wondered anew who was the lady in Oxford Street, the one he'd claimed was not his wife. Was she another person Daniel was deceiving? Or was he watching her, as he'd done with Sir Lionel?

He'd said Sir Lionel had been meeting with certain people and reporting what they told him to Daniel, in exchange for Daniel ... doing what? Not telling the police Sir Lionel was spying, or plotting crimes, or whatever it was? Who were these bad people Daniel feared would hurt me? Or was *Daniel* the bad person, and whoever Sir Lionel had been in league with were on the side of good?

No, I couldn't believe that last. Sir Lionel had been mean-spirited, rather stupid, and cunning at the same time. He could not be up to any good no matter what he did.

Grace's idea about the sugar caster interested me, though. I could imagine someone at the table stealthily pocketing the caster full of poison, meaning to replace it on the table with one without poison. But they hadn't managed it and had to stash the clean caster in the plant. Because the people at the table had started feeling ill and rushed away? Or had the person trying to replace the caster been interrupted by John or Sally coming to clear the table?

But then, why had Mrs. Watkins claimed there was no sugar caster at all? Copley had been too drunk to wait at table that night ... or had he been? Had he crept upstairs and set the poison on the table, removing it again when Mrs. Watkins's back was turned?

There was nothing for it. I had to speak with Copley.

This entailed finding out where he was being kept, now that he'd been arrested for stealing Sir Lionel's wine and silver. I regretted hastening away from Daniel so abruptly, because Daniel would know.

I knew I'd never find Daniel if I wanted to—even if I waited outside the house in Oxford Street, there was nothing to say he'd return there—so I hunted for James. Sure enough, James was lurking around Sir Lionel's house with the excuse of doing odd jobs in the neighborhood. Daniel had told him to continue watching the place, he said.

When I told him I needed to speak to his father, James nodded and told me to wait inside Sir Lionel's house. He handed me the key, said he'd send Daniel to me, and ran off with the energy of youth.

I entered through the back door and went to the only place in that house I was comfortable, the kitchen. The familiarity of it wrapped around me, wanting to draw me back.

Too bad Sir Lionel had been such a terrible master. Perhaps when his heir moved in, he'd need a cook. The heir would be of sunnier disposition, appreciate my food, and not make strange demands on me or disgust me with amorous advances. Miracles could happen.

To pass the time, I went into the butler's pantry and looked through the silver in the glass wall cabinets. All was as it should be, except of course for the missing pieces that Copley had stolen. The settings all matched — the Leigh-Bradburys had used the same silversmith for years.

I frowned. I went to the housekeeper's room, fetched her keys, and returned to the pantry to open the cases. I studied the silver plates, candlesticks, and serving pieces like the chafing pan, a footed dish in the shape of a shell, the cruet stand, and a wine bucket. These pieces were larger, difficult to carry off without being noticed, which was no doubt why Copley had left them. Copley had taken smaller pieces — salt cellar, cups, spoons, finger bowls.

In a drawer below the glass-fronted shelves I found pots of silver polish and rags, as well as the velvet-lined boxes for the place settings. There were two unopened store-bought pots of polish with pink labels. A third pink-labeled pot had been opened, as had a pot of homemade polish—washing soda and salt, which the polisher would wet with lemon juice or vinegar before rubbing on the silver.

I took a delicate sniff of the homemade polish then closed the lid and slipped it into my pocket.

"Kat?" An alarmed voice was calling with Daniel's deep timbre. "Are you here? Where are you?"

I locked the cabinets, not hurrying, returned the keys to the housekeeper's room, and made my way to the kitchen.

Daniel breathed out when he saw me. "Damn it all, Kat ..."

"Please do not swear at me," I said calmly. "And I am *Mrs. Holloway*."

"Why did you have James find me?" The irritation and anger did not leave his voice.

"To take me to see Copley. I assume you know where they've put him?"

Daniel gave me a nod, his look hard. "At the moment, in hospital. He's seriously ill."

My brows lifted, my heart beating faster. "Oh, dear. In that case, I must speak to him at once."

***

Copley had been jailed at Newgate, but had been taken to the infirmary. He lay in a bed in a long, mostly empty ward. The ward was gray and unfriendly, windowless and gloomy, but it was a step better than the common cells. Just.

Copley looked terrible. His face was as gray as the walls and had a yellow cast to it. His entire body trembled, and when we approached, he turned over in his bed and vomited into the bucket at his bedside.

The air around him stank. I took a handkerchief from my bag and pressed it to my nose.

"Copley," Daniel said. "Sorry to see you so wretched, old chap."

Daniel was in his scruffy clothes again, holding his cloth cap. He looked like a carter or furniture mover, come to help the neat and tidy woman at his side. When we'd entered the jail, however, we'd been treated deferentially and led to Copley without question.

"What d'ye want?" Copley rasped. "Let me die in peace. Why'd ye bring *her* here?"

"You might not die," I said cheerfully. "Mrs. Fuller managed to recover. I imagine because someone politely replenished the sugar on her tart for her instead of making her shake it on herself. *You* probably only held the caster long enough to hide it in the plant pot, and luckily, you wore gloves."

Daniel glanced at me, perplexed, and

Copley blinked. "What th' devil are ye going on about, woman?"

"It is simple," I said. "*You* took the sugar caster from the table." I pointed a gloved finger at Copley. "You did so when you thought no one was looking. Maybe when you and John were clearing up? Or John was clearing up while you helped yourself to any leftover food and drink." Those plates had been *very* clean when they'd returned to the kitchen. "You didn't have time to do anything with the caster—perhaps someone nearly caught you with it. Or you hid it when I sent John for the police and was downstairs dressing, fearing it would be found on you or in your room if there was a search. You stole many of the smaller pieces that night and stashed them to fetch later. Why not the sugar caster too?"

"Yes, all right," Copley growled. "I plucked the bloody thing off the table when I saw it, but Mrs. Watkins and John were right on top of me, so I hid it in the plant."

"Why not take it back downstairs with the other pieces?" I asked. I thought I knew the answer, but I wanted Copley to say it in front of Daniel.

"Because it weren't ours," Copley said angrily. "Not Sir Lionel's. I thought maybe them Fullers brought their own caster with them and forgot and left it behind. John would return it to our cabinet, not knowing the difference, then Mrs. Interfering Watkins would find it and send it back to Mrs. Fuller."

Daniel listened with a sparkle in his eyes. "You're saying the caster didn't belong in the house?"

Copley wet his lips, but he was losing strength, so I spoke for him. Copley really was a pitiful wretch.

"The sugar caster was made by a different silversmith," I explained. "If you check its hallmark, you'll see. Sir Lionel's family has used the same silversmith down the generations. All the pieces match. But I advise you, Mr. McAdam, that if you do handle the caster again, or your chemist does, please wear gloves. And ask your chemist to check the contents of *this*."

I brought out the small pot of homemade silver polish, which was still wrapped in my handkerchief. I set pot and handkerchief into Daniel's outstretched hands—which were covered with thick workman's gloves. He handled the pot with respect, but looked at me in bewilderment.

I turned back to Copley. "Did you or John ever use homemade silver polish?"

"No." Copley's voice was weak. "I used the stuff from Finch's. Much better for keeping off the tarnish."

"That's what I thought. Thank you, Copley. I do hope you mend soon."

"Would if the buggers in this place would give me a decent drop to drink."

I gave Copley a nod, pleased with him, and excited by what he'd told me. "That is possibly true." I said. "Shall we depart, Mr. McAdam?"

***

Daniel insisted on hiring a hansom cab to take us back through London. I didn't like to sit so close to him in the small vehicle, but rain had begun to pelt down, and I would have to endure the annoyance for a dry ride to King Street.

Daniel began speaking as though we had no tension between us. "You believe the poison was *on* the caster itself?" he asked. "Coating it?"

I nodded. "Test the homemade silver polish I gave you. If it were rubbed into a paste onto the caster, anyone lifting it would get it on their fingers. Then if they ate bits of food—eventually, they would ingest enough of whatever it is to make them ill. Or the poison could sink in through the skin. I'm not certain about that. Perhaps it would work by both means."

"Mrs. Watkins didn't take ill," Daniel pointed out. "If she handled the caster ... though she insists it wasn't there. What about poor John? We need to find him."

"John always wore gloves when waiting at table. Mrs. Watkins did not, but she was right as rain when I saw her yesterday, obviously not ill from poison. It is bad manners for ladies and gentlemen to wear gloves at table, and so the diners had no protection."

"But Copley?" Daniel frowned as he puzzled things out. "Why did it take him some time to become ill? Butlers wear gloves while they're setting up or serving at table, as footmen do."

He knew a lot about butlers, did he? "True, but I've watched how Copley sometimes takes his gloves off."

I demonstrated, delicately tugging at the fingers of one glove with my teeth, loosening it before drawing it off. "This is why I do not believe Copley poisoned Sir Lionel and the Fullers. If he'd coated the caster with poison, he'd have been more careful."

Daniel made a sound of agreement. "So, Copley is a thief, not a murderer."

This wouldn't help Copley much—he'd stolen items of high value and might be hanged for it, or perhaps transported if someone spoke up for him. Poor drunken fool.

"I will visit Mrs. Fuller again," Daniel said briskly. "And see if the caster came from her household. It is still possible *she* did the poisoning—or someone employed by her at her instruction."

I didn't think so, but I said nothing. Mrs. Fuller would have been certain to take the caster away and dispose of it, I would think, even if she'd deliberately made herself ill. The caster would not have been there for Copley to try to steal.

When the hansom stopped in front of my boardinghouse, I began to descend, but Daniel caught my hand and drew me back.

"I want you to take the post I spoke about," he said. "I will tell Clarendon's housekeeper to expect you for an interview."

I'd had enough. I jerked from his grasp but remained in the hansom. "Let me speak plainly, Mr. McAdam. You have deceived me at every turn. Believe me, I am vexed with myself for letting you. However, I have made my way in this world on my own for a number of years now, and I will continue to do so. I am grateful for what you have done for me—I sincerely thank you for saving me from the magistrates—but I have my life to get on with. I am not a silly woman; I will take every precaution for my own safety."

How this speech affected Daniel, I could not tell. He only regarded me with calm eyes—the eyes I'd once thought so handsome—and did not change expression.

"Very well," he said, his voice cool. "Then I will bid you good night."

I made a noise of exasperation. The least he could do was look contrite. He'd withdrawn, the affable Daniel gone, a cool shell in his place.

So be it.

My heart ached as I scrambled down from the hansom and made for my lodgings. I'd fallen for Daniel McAdam, whoever he was, but that Daniel did not exist. This was the painful truth I had to accept, and continue with my life.

Chapter Ten

I saw nothing of Daniel or James for the next few days. I unpacked my box at the boardinghouse and visited my agency to find another post.

Difficult this time of year. Families of the big Mayfair houses were mostly gone to the country, and those who hadn't left already were packing to head out for the hunting and shooting seasons.

After that would be Christmas and New Years', the majority of society families not returning until spring. So many already had cooks installed in their London houses, cooks who went on preparing meals for the skeleton staff in the winter or for renters.

The minor gentry also went to the country or else they wanted a woman who'd plunk a joint of beef and watery potatoes in front of the family every evening and naught else. At least when Sir Lionel had been baiting me, he'd stretched my abilities and let me create meals worthy of a master chef.

I came away from the agency the days I visited it depressed and disgruntled. I might have to swallow my pride, hunt up Daniel, and take the post at Berkeley Square.

I did make a journey south of the river to see Sally, who had indeed returned home. She flew at me and hugged me, having believed me already convicted and hanged even in this short time. She was not much help, though. She knew nothing of the sugar caster or of the extra box of polish. She wasn't allowed to polish the silver, only to wash plates and crockery. The sugar caster never came near her sink, and she never went to the dining room or Sir Lionel's library.

She had nothing but honest innocence and confusion in her eyes, and I came away, unenlightened. She was about to start a new post in another kitchen, she said, thankfully. Her family needed her wages.

James arrived at the boardinghouse to visit me about a week after that. He did not actually come to the back door and request to speak with me; he simply skulked about in the street until I went out.

He told me with his usual cheerfulness that Daniel had found the footman, John, who was in Dorset, as I'd suspected. John was in raring good health, thank the Lord. Daniel had asked John to give him the gloves he'd used when serving that last meal and taken them away.

Daniel's chemist had tested the caster and found it coated with arsenic. That sort of thing could seep through the fingers or be eaten, with the same result—horrible illness and probable death. It could happen quickly, or take time—there must have been much of the stuff on the caster. Mrs. Fuller had indeed been very lucky.

When James finished giving me this news, I decided to ask him what I had been wondering about him point blank. "James, does it bother you that your father is not what he seems?"

The lad considered my question, his father's brown eyes in his smudged young face regarding me calmly. "I lived with the charwoman, as I said. She had a man also boarding in her house who wanted to use me as his fancy boy and beat me regular when I refused. One day, me dad—Mr. McAdam, as ye know him—came along, had the man arrested, and took me away."

James rubbed under his lower lip. "At the time, I thought me dad were the same—a man what liked boys, only he had a few more coins to rub together. But he got angry when I accused him of that. He told me he was my pa and would take care of me now. He showed me how we looked alike, and he knew all about my ma—may she rest in peace—and eventually, I believed him."

He shrugged. "Dad comes and goes all the time. I never asked where. If he has a posh house and family besides me—well some gents do, don't they? A house for the wife and one for the mistress? A house for his legitimate family, and one for his by-blows?"

I listened with mixed emotions. Daniel had been good to rescue James and make sure he was well looked after. On the other hand, James made a true point about gentlemen leading double lives.

"Thank you for telling me," was all I could think to say.

James grinned. "Don't look so primmed up, missus. I've always known I weren't the Prince of Wales. I'm a gent's bastard, Dad's kind to me, and I get by."

Would that I could take such a casual attitude. Daniel indeed led a double life—a triple one, perhaps.

However, I'd had my fill of men who did whatever they pleased, never mind who they trampled over or cast aside along their way, uncaring of how many women bore their children and were left to raise them on their own.

"Thank you, James, for telling me the news. I know you had no need to keep me informed."

"Thought you'd like to know. Dad said you'd be interested but didn't think you'd want to see him."

"He thought right." I dug into my pocket and pulled out a coin, but James lifted his hands and stepped away.

"Don't insult me now," he said. "I did ya a favor." He renewed his grin, tipped his cap, and jogged away into the busy London street.

***

When next I had the time, I made my way to Pimlico to visit Mrs. Watkins. Daniel might be questioning Mrs. Fuller and her staff up and down, but I wanted to quiz Mrs. Watkins again about that bloody sugar caster.

I met her in the sitting room of her sister's boardinghouse. She was having the same difficulty as I in landing a new post, but I imagined she'd find one before I did. More Londoners needed housekeepers while they were away than wanted to bother with cooks, especially cooks of my calibre.

"Perhaps I should open a restaurant," I said. "Though where I'd find the funds for such an endeavor, I have no idea."

"You'd soon tire of it," Mrs. Watkins said with conviction. "Instead of cooking for one table that complains, there'd be many tables complaining all night. My sister ran a restaurant for a time, but gave it up for a boardinghouse. An easier task, she says."

The maid brought tea, Mrs. Watkins poured, and we drank.

"Are you certain about that sugar caster?" I asked after we'd sipped.

Mrs. Watkins coughed, set down her teacup, and wiped her mouth with a napkin. "The one you asked me about before? Of course I am certain, Mrs. Holloway. I would have noticed it."

I took another sip of tea. The service was elegant, delicate porcelain with sprays of pink roses on it. No silver in sight, except for the small teaspoons. "You see, Mrs. Watkins, John says he saw the caster there. So did Mrs. Fuller. And Copley stole it, the wretch, hiding it to take away later. So you must have either been extremely unobservant, or are telling me an untruth."

"Well, you may believe what you like." Mrs. Watkins's indignation made her cup tremble as she picked it up again. "John is not bright, Copley only saw a silver piece he could steal, and Mrs. Fuller is obviously lying. *She* must have poisoned the meal, perhaps in the wine. They poured that themselves."

I sipped tea again and gave a little shrug. "It may be as you say."

"I will tell you what I think." Mrs. Watkins leaned forward, the cameo at her throat moving. "That delivery man, Daniel McAdam, as was always hanging about the house. He must have had something to do with it. There's something not quite pukka about him."

I nodded, saying nothing.

I had, in fact, considered Daniel as a suspect. He certainly was good at misleading. If he'd been watching Sir Lionel as he'd said, having Sir Lionel report to him, perhaps he'd begun to see the man as a danger.

Sir Lionel could report to these bad people that Daniel was requiring Sir Lionel to give him information. To shut Sir Lionel's mouth, Daniel poisoned the caster and got it to the table somehow — perhaps through Copley. When I was arrested for his deed, he felt remorse and decided to help me.

I had not pursued this line of thought, because my emotions about Daniel were jumbled, and I refused to trust my own judgment where he was concerned, at least not for the moment.

The maid brought in a stack of clean plates

and began to lay them on the long table on the other side room. Tea would be served to the other tenants soon, and I ought to go.

I rose, but instead of leaving, I walked to the table. The maid was setting at one end a silver cream pot, sugar bowl with lumps of sugar in it, and sugar caster for the finer sugar that would be sprinkled on tea cakes.

I took up the caster, turned it over, and examined the hallmark, finding it identical to the one on the caster we'd found at Sir Lionel's.

The maid, ignoring me, moved to the other end of the table and laid out a twin of the cream pot and sugar bowl—two sets for a large number of diners.

I moved to her, lifting the second sugar bowl as though admiring it. "Do you have two of everything?"

"We do," the maid said, continuing to lay out forks and spoons. "It's not posh silver, but it's nice looking, I think. Except for the second sugar caster. That's gone missing."

I turned around to Mrs. Watkins, the caster and sugar bowl in my hand. Her face had become a peculiar shade of green.

"So the caster *didn't* come from Mrs. Fuller," I said to Mrs. Watkins. "It came from here."

A number of things happened at once. The maid looked up in surprise, her expression holding nothing but bewilderment. The door to the parlor opened and Mrs. Watkins's sister rushed inside. Mrs. Watkins left the sofa and came at me in a run.

Certain Mrs. Watkins meant to attack me, I held up my hands protectively, the silver pieces still in them. Her sister, Mrs. Herbert, came after her.

At the last minute, Mrs. Watkins swung around, putting herself across me like a shield. "Leave her be," she said swiftly. "Mrs. Holloway knows nothing. She'll say nothing."

I stared in surprise at Mrs. Herbert, the sister, and then realized that I'd seen her before—in a photo in Sir Lionel Leigh-Bradbury's library. She was older now—that photo had been of a fresh-faced young woman. I recognized the straight nose and regular features, the happy eyes of that girl. Now cynicism and age lined her face.

"Who are you?" I blurted out.

"I was his affianced," Mrs. Herbert snapped. "I broke the engagement when I realized what a parsimonious, evil little man he was. I married a better man. And then Sir Lionel ruined him. My Charles died in disgrace and penury, because of *him*."

Thoughts rearranged themselves rapidly in my head. Mrs. Watkins swearing the sugar caster hadn't been there, John swearing it had, and Copley plucking it from the table after supper and hiding it.

"You gave Copley the poisoned polish and told him he must use it, didn't you?" I asked Mrs. Herbert. "Paying him a nice sum for his services? I have no idea if he knew what it was—he might have been more careful if he did. Then you told Copley to carry the caster to the table. I shouldn't wonder if you promised him he could have it. If his greed made him ill or killed him, so much the better."

Mrs. Watkins, whom I'd never seen less than dignified, shook with tears. "Oh, Letty. How could you?"

"I have no remorse," Mrs. Herbert said, her head high. "Sir Lionel held a minor government post, and he filled enough ears with lies to have my Charles investigated for treason. The case dragged on and on until Charles sickened and died. He was proved innocent in the end, but too late for him. Sir Lionel killed my husband, as good as stabbing him through the heart."

"Is that why you stuck my carving knife into him?" I asked. "To make a point?"

Mrs. Herbert looked momentarily puzzled. "I never went into the house. Or near it."

Of course she hadn't. That way, nothing would connect her to the crime. The damning sugar caster would be taken away by Copley, cleaned and sold. No one would know it came from Mrs. Herbert's house.

But Copley had bungled it, lost his nerve, possibly when John had come to clear the table, and stuffed the caster into the rubber tree's pot to be retrieved later. He'd been caught going back into the house to find it and the other pieces he'd stashed, while the poison was working inside him to make him sick.

I could picture Copley creeping up to Sir Lionel's library, where the man sat, dead already, to stick my carving knife into his back to both ensure the man was dead and throw blame upon me. The scullery maid had heard him moving about and came to fetch me, so Copley had to flee back upstairs and pretend to be just waking up, no time to pick up the caster.

And then the house had been full of police, rambling all over it for the next day or so, and Copley had made himself scarce to wait until the house was empty again. He couldn't have known that I'd be released from prison and Daniel would be watching to catch him.

"How could you?" Mrs. Watkins repeated. "A second man died, and his wife was taken ill."

"Copley is ill as well," I put in.

Mrs. Watkins went on, ignoring me. "Any of us in that house could have touched that piece or used the polish, Letty. John, the scullery maid, Mrs. Holloway, even me."

Mrs. Herbert scowled. "Would serve you right for working for that monster, taking his money."

"I did it for *you*." Mrs. Watkins began to sob. "I was trying to discover how to ruin him. For you!"

Mrs. Herbert paused at that, then her expression hardened. "I am not sorry that Sir Lionel is dead. My Charles has been avenged."

With that, she came at me in a rage. Mrs. Watkins caught her sister before she could reach me. I was about to spring forward and give Mrs. Herbert a good thump, when the woman's heel caught on the carpet, and she collapsed to the sofa.

The strength went out of her, her face growing pale, her pupils narrowing to pinpricks. Her breath came in gasps, full-blown hysteria on its way.

Mrs. Watkins sank down beside her sister, crying as well, the two of them becoming a wailing mess. The maid looked on in shock.

I put down the silver pieces, opened my bag, removed my smelling salts, and went to the two ladies, waving the little bottle under their noses.

Mrs. Watkins sat up abruptly, but Mrs. Herbert remained slumped against the sofa's back, breathing hard. I could see the innocent beauty she'd been before she'd been trapped by Sir Lionel. Sir Lionel had been an odious man, and I couldn't help believe he'd been justly punished.

On the other hand, there was nothing to say Mrs. Herbert wouldn't simply become a crazed poisoner. She'd not worried a bit about the rest of us being sickened as well, from the Fullers—people she'd never met—to her own sister. In addition, I'd almost been tried for the crime, my fate, certain hanging.

I took from my bag the vial of laudanum I'd brought for the purpose of subduing Mrs. Watkins—because I'd thought it she who'd poisoned Sir Lionel and the Fullers. While Mrs. Herbert lay gasping like a fish, I held her nose and poured the laudanum into her mouth, forcing her to swallow.

Mrs. Watkins was still crying, but she made no move to stop me. Perhaps she too worried that her sister had gone a bit mad.

After that, I strode out of the room and out of the house, in search of a constable. I nearly ran into James, who was hovering near the railings that separated the house from the street.

"Gracious, what are you doing here?" I asked him.

"Following you," James said. "Dad told me to. You all right?"

"No. Fetch a constable, will you? I've found the poisoner of Sir Lionel Leigh-Bradbury."

I had the satisfaction of seeing young James gape at me before his face cleared, and he beamed.

"I knew you could do it!" he shouted, then was away in a flash, running to find the nearest constable.

Chapter Eleven

I was never certain what happened to Mrs. Herbert. She was arrested, likely shut in to the same kind of cell I had been, her trial scheduled.

I walked away from Mrs. Watkins, her house, Sir Lionel's, and all the rest of it. I visited my daughter again, holding her close until I could breathe once more.

I knew, though, that I'd never be free of it in my heart. I'd lived in a house where a man had been poisoned and died, and I'd condemned a woman to death for it. She'd go to the crowded cell in Newgate where I had waited in fear, only she would not be set free.

I'd met Daniel, half fallen in love with him and had been sorely deceived by him. After Grace's father deserted me, I'd vowed I'd never let a man trick me again, and yet the first fine pair of eyes I saw, I was off. I badly needed to curb these tendencies.

My agency did at last find me a post a few weeks later, in a large house in Richmond. The lady of the house had heard of my cooking from my previous employer, Mrs. Pauling, and was happy to have me.

Richmond was a bit far from my daughter for my taste, but the pay was good, I had an ample number of days out, and it was only a short train ride to the heart of London. Perhaps I could bring Grace out to Richmond to visit me, and we could walk along the river and see the sights. She'd like that.

The house was a good place, with the kitchen run efficiently—even more so once I'd taken command.

One cold winter day, as I went over a list of what I needed to prepare supper, a gentleman walked, unannounced, into the kitchen.

This house had a large servants' hall across the passage from the big kitchen, its own laundry rooms, housekeeper's parlor, a butler's pantry far larger than the closet-sized one at Sir Lionel's, and a fairly cozy bedroom down the corridor for me. The corridor and rooms were always teeming with the servants needed to tend a large household.

The gentleman could only have entered the servants' area by coming down the stairs that led to the main house, or in through the scullery door from outside. Either way, he'd have been noticed and politely questioned by the three strapping footman, the butler—who was a proper butler and not a wastrel like Copley—and the housekeeper, long before he reached the kitchen.

However, no one seemed to have stopped him, and the entire staff, when I looked around, was startlingly absent.

The gentleman was Daniel. He was dressed in what I would say were middle-class clothes—not so posh as the ones I'd seen him wear in Oxford Street, but not so scruffy as his work trousers and boots. His hair was tamed but not pomaded, a bit rumpled, but combed flat. He set a hat and pair of leather gloves on my kitchen table and rested one hip on the tabletop as though perfectly at home.

"It is good to see you, Kat."

I waited a few heartbeats until I was certain my voice would not crack. "Good day, Mr. McAdam. How is James?"

"He is well. Working." A wry look entered his eyes. "That is, when he's not off doing what he bloody well pleases."

"Ah." I knew Daniel wanted me to smile, so I did not. "What brings you to

Richmond?"

"Hope." Daniel's gaze fixed on me. "I want us to be friends again, Kat. Like before."

"Oh, do you now?" I laid down the list of foodstuffs and clicked the pencil next to it. "Well, I'm certain *you* would feel much better if I agreed. If I forgive you, you will be much relieved."

Daniel lost his forced, polite look. "Damn it, Kat."

He came to me and pulled me around to face him, holding my arms with his hard hands. I felt the solid lip of the table behind me as I looked up into his angry face. Daniel's eyes had a dangerous glint in them. I had no idea what he was about to do, but I lifted my chin.

"Threatening me will not help your cause," I said crisply. "Remember, I'm a dab hand with a knife."

Rage turned to frustrated amusement. Daniel cupped my face with a firm hand, leaned down, and kissed my mouth. "I could fall in love with you, Kat Holloway," he said, his voice low.

My heart fluttered like a dove's wings. However, I refused to let him know that I could fall stupidly in love with him in return.

"The lady in Oxford Street might be a bit put out," I said. "Mr. McAdam dallying with a cook? Not the done thing."

Daniel made an impatient noise. "The lady in Oxford Street is—was—an assignment. Like Sir Lionel. Both of those are finished."

"Are they?" My heart beat thickly, and I could barely think. The kiss had been a rather fine one, Daniel stood close, and my coherence was running away. "You should be on to the next thing then."

"I am. Unfortunately. But I had to ..." Daniel trailed off, his fingers on my face softening. "I wanted to make sure you were well, Kat."

"I am," I said, surprised my voice was so steady. "As you can see. This is a fine kitchen."

"It is." Daniel drew a breath, lowered his hand, and deliberately stepped away from me. "What is it you prepare tonight, Mrs. Holloway?"

I had to consult my list, because my menu had just gone clean out of my head. "Beef bourguignon. Sorrel soup, fish in white wine, and lemon tart to finish."

"Ah, Kat, you make my mouth water." Daniel kissed his fingers to me, slanting me his wicked look. "If I happen to be passing in my delivery wagon after supper, might I beg a scrap or two to sustain me?"

He wanted to transform back to the Daniel I knew best, did he? "What about this?" I asked, waving my hand at his suit. "This ... banker's clerk, or whatever you are? Where will he be?"

"Gone after this evening, I'm afraid."

"I see. Will I ever, perchance, meet the real Daniel McAdam?"

Daniel lost his smile. "Perhaps one day. Yes, definitely one day, I'll bare my soul to you, Kat. I promise."

My voice went quiet. "Will I like what I see when you do?"

"I don't know." The words rang true. "But I believe I am willing to risk it."

I had no idea what to say to that, or what I ought to do. Forgive him? Turn my back on him forever? Do neither, and go on with him as though nothing had happened?

One thing was certain—there was far more to Daniel than met the eye. I was curious enough, blast it, to want to learn everything I could about the man.

"In that case," I said, taking up my pencil again. "If you are not too late, I might save back a bit of lemon tart for you."

Daniel's smile returned. "I would enjoy that very much."

We shared a look. Daniel took up his hat and gloves, giving me a bow.

"You have more skills than cooking," he said. "Perhaps you will help me on another hunt someday."

I shivered. "Indeed no. Once was enough for me."

"Was it?" Daniel carefully pulled on his gloves. "We'll see. Good afternoon, Mrs. Holloway. I look forward to speaking with you again."

And I, you, I wanted to say, but held my tongue. "Good afternoon, Mr. McAdam."

He shot me a grin, came back to me, kissed me on the lips, and strode out, whistling.

End

A Matter of Honor

A Matter of Honor

London, 1820

"You are a drunken lout," my brother, Sir Frederick Archer, shouted at me in his fog-gloomed sitting room in Berkeley Square the Michaelmas after the *drohner* had disappeared. "Gin-soaked and pox-brained. What luck that Bonaparte has been defeated at last—I wager the King's army would not take you now."

"I do not have the pox," I said with dignity. Alas, my words slurred, because I was, as accused, gin-soaked.

Margery, his wife, cringed in a chair by the window, pretending interest in her needlework. She had the complexion of a tallow candle, her hair a golden color those with very fair hair in youth sometimes acquired.

I, Robert Archer, the younger brother, had paid a call on her, my dear sister-in-law, to ask if she could spare a few shillings until my next pay packet. But my brother had come upon us before I was able to make my request and had taken the opportunity to lecture.

When he paused for breath, I said, "You are angry, and blame me for losing the *drohner*. I did not steal the bloody thing." But I'd had it in my care when it had vanished three months ago, and that thought haunted me every moment of every day. The *drohner* was shared between family members, passing from house to house. It had been in mine when it went missing.

"You *displayed* it," Frederick snapped. "In your front room to your drunken friends — dear God. You broke a sacred family trust."

"It is not unique." I made the excuse I'd been making since the thing had gone. "My friends had seen one before — every gentleman's family has one. None are secret, for all they're locked away like the crown jewels." The speech taxed my sodden brain, and I dropped to the nearest chair, my legs too shaky to hold me.

"Even the king has one, Frederick," Margery said timidly.

My brother swung on his wife, dark eyes ablaze. "What he has is false, created on a pretense to make his family seem more connected to English ones. Ours had the lines, the power, the magic of our ancestors for seven hundred years. Now gone. Because of *his* carelessness."

He thrust a finger at me. Behind him, Margery gave me a helpless look from her light brown eyes, which I returned. We both writhed under my brother's thumb. Frederick had been a strong, muscular man—now he was running to fat, his face round and red, his brown hair lank. I'd look like him before long unless I had a care. At the same time his waistcoat and frock coat hung in loose folds on him as though he'd lost weight since the *drohner* had gone, his breeches wrinkled about his knees.

"And he has made no effort to retrieve it," Frederick carried on. "Three months since it has gone, and he has done *nothing*. He is not fit to belong to our family. I do not even know why you are here, Robert."

I did not tell him I'd come for money. Margery had enough misery without her husband knowing she occasionally let me touch her for blunt.

I pried myself out of the chair, said polite good-byes to Margery, and escaped the house. But I had left empty-handed.

I'd have to sell my commission, I reflected as I walked along the rain-soaked pavement of Berkeley Square. Night had fallen, and the golden smudge of gaslights behind the fog did little to light the way.

I had hung onto my commission in part to annoy my brother but mostly because it meant something to me. A lieutenant's pay did not carry far, and my father had left me nothing. My brother had inherited everything—the baronetcy, land, money, houses—but my father hadn't felt any obligation to provide for his younger son. I had nothing but my pay packet, meager as it was, and my rank, my own form of honor.

But my brother was wrong. I had been searching for the *drohner*. I cared as much for it as did Frederick, and I bled with guilt. Frederick was right—I should have looked after the bloody thing better.

A *drohner*, in its most basic sense, is a square of polished black stone, pretty to look upon, but it is much more than that. Every *drohner* holds its family's power. Every son puts his hand on his family's *drohner* the day of his majority and swears to protect it. Every dying man holds it between his hands, giving to it his magics to carry to the next generation. The *drohner* was kept in a place of pride in the household, hidden from all eyes but the family's, and its magic protected the family and gave it honor.

Other families, old and powerful ones,

had lost *drohners* or had seen them destroyed by their enemies. Those families had dwindled, faded into nothingness. I wondered how much time would pass before our family suffered the same fate.

Margery, in her ten-year marriage to Frederick, had been brought to bed of one child, stillborn, and had borne no more. Frederick made her feel it keenly. And I, unmarried, childless—as far as I knew— stumbled through the streets of London without tuppence in my pocket.

Which is why the attack surprised me. Why should ruffians bother to rob me?

I heard the swift tramp of feet, then a heavy blow landed on the back of my neck— not a fist, a cosh. My legs buckled and the pavement rose up to knock the wind from me. The owner of a huge boot kicked me in the ribs. Another kick, from a smaller boot but no less painful, landed on the small of my back. A pair of beefy hands shoved my face to the cobbles, and fists pummeled me. Blood spattered from my parted lips as I tried to explain I had no money, no watch, nothing.

Abruptly the boot vanished from my back, the hands from my neck. I took a long breath, blood clogging my nose. I raised my head, but blackness danced before me, and I fell, hard, to the pavement again.

I awoke, facedown in my own bed. My head throbbed, my tongue lay like lead in my mouth.

Another drunken binge, I decided. Then I saw that my hands, which were wrapped in bandages, lay on either side of my head like leprous slugs.

The clink of glass on glass came to me. I turned my head to see, in the light of a lone candle, a slim woman pouring liquid from a decanter into a glass. I prayed it was brandy.

The woman had blond hair, a deeper golden than her high-waisted gown, wound into a heavy braid on the crown of her head. Her eyes were dark, nearly black. Otherwise, she was ordinary, with a face pretty but not extraordinarily so, a trim figure, not heavily buxom. Her dress was cotton, floating lace, clean and mended.

In outward appearance, she looked like a woman I might brush by in the street or see in the markets or at Exeter 'Change. But her eyes, deep and black, the irises swallowing her pupils, betrayed her. I would never in my life forget those haunted eyes I'd seen a few years ago as she'd implored me, from behind a pile of crates, to take her child from her and go.

I forced open my dry lips. *"You."*

She came to me and slipped a long-fingered hand under my head. Alas, the glass held only water. I drank deeply, suddenly burning with thirst.

"You did me a good turn once," she said. "I vowed to do you one, if I could."

Her voice was smooth, still with calm. Quite unlike the terrified tremor it had held that night in Covent Garden.

I'd only been *half*-drunk that night. She'd crouched in the shadows, blood all over her gown, and she'd thrust the squalling bundle at me. "Please, take her. Take her far away."

I'd stared stupidly at the screwed up face and closed eyes, the pink lips drawn back from gums in a silent cry of hunger.

"Where on earth am I to take her?"

She'd only looked at me as she laid the bundle in my arms, her eyes pools of terror. I'd assumed her a game girl, gotten with child by some flat, hiding in the corner for her lying-in. Her desperation stabbed me so deep that I had to look away to shut it out.

The babe had squirmed, its mouth seeking nourishment in the faded braid of my uniform. When I'd looked back for the young woman, she'd vanished into the shadows, leaving me alone with her child.

I'd taken the babe to a woman called Lizzie in St. Martin's Lane. She'd been a wet nurse and had a healthy brood of her own. Without questioning me, she'd taken the bundle into her competent hands and sent her oldest boy scurrying away to find a girl she knew who'd just birthed. The son returned with the bleary-eyed girl in tow, and soon the tiny life was happily suckling at her bosom.

Lizzie and I had then stolen a few moments together in the cellar while her husband snored on in the kitchen surrounded by the fruit of his loins. From time to time, during the last year or two, I'd followed my curiosity back to the house where the babe still lived, adopted by the large-hearted Lizzie into her own ample family.

I finished the water, and she lowered me down on my stomach again. I'd been far too tired to turn over, even to drink.

"Did you bring me home by yourself?" I croaked at her. I hardly thought it likely. She looked much better than when I'd last seen her, her cheeks pale but not deathly so, her gown whole and unstained, her movements competent and easy. Robust, yes, but not robust enough to carry me here without help.

She set the empty glass on my bedside table. "I did, yes."

I looked at her slim arms and tried to smile. "You couldn't drag a cat home, miss, let alone a drunken lieutenant no better than he ought to be."

Her hand landed with a suddenness on

my neck, and she pinned me to the bed with hideous strength. My face smashed into the ticking and I could not draw breath.

"Had you not guessed?" she asked.

Watery fear washed my bones. I struggled against the pressure on my neck, which was no more use than struggling against an oak tree. Once on a battlefield in Portugal, a French soldier had risen from the scrub not three feet from me and pointed his pistol at my forehead. I'd stared into that round, black barrel of oblivion and smelled death.

Upon firing, the pistol had kicked faintly to the left, and the ball had whizzed by my ear. The French soldier had cursed mightily then died with my sergeant's bayonet in his stomach.

That fear was nothing to what I felt now.

She was a night-slayer. They crawled London's seedy darkness late at night, feeding on the blood of the helpless, the lone wayfarer, those who had nowhere to turn. They took the old, the young, the healthy, the sick, all without discrimination. They'd infested the city from time to time in the past, until the terror-stricken citizenry had demanded they be rooted out. The last infestation had been in 1750, when a pack had descended into St. Giles and ruled there until the King's army had been sent to drive them away. There had been no infestation since then—nearly seventy years ago now—though reports from time to time of night-slayer-like killings had led to panic and every Bow Street Runner brought in to hunt the slayer.

Night-slayers did not die, except from starvation. They shunned the light, but it did not harm them. They were vermin, skulking in the night and shadows like rats, but they could also look like ordinary people—a game girl, a beggar, a lamp-lighter, or a blond young woman who'd saved me from robbery tonight.

"Are you going to kill me?" I asked, my voice weak with fear.

She released me so abruptly that I slumped into the ticking, spent and exhausted.

"I could have killed you where you lay in the street," she said. "I did not."

I turned my head to stare at her, then a thought struck me. "God's truth, that child was not a night-slayer, was it?" I had given it to Lizzie and her family—what had I done?

She looked, to my surprise, amused. "Night-slayers are made, not born. She is as alive as you are. Why do you think I begged you to take her away? I did not wish to harm her in my hunger. I still have a heart that feels and grieves." She pinned me with her hard gaze. "Is she safe?"

"Yes. I took her to —"

"I know where you took her. Is she well?"

I nodded into the mattress. "She is. She has seven brothers and sisters and cream and porridge every day. She was walking the last time I saw her."

Tears shone in the dark eyes for a brief instant, but vanished so quickly I might have imagined them. She turned from the bed and started for the door — I realized she was leaving. Just like that, no good-byes, no more conversation.

"Do you have a name?" I called after her.

"No." At the door, she paused, her hand on the handle. "*You* are Robert Sebastian Archer of the 26th Rifles. In number 24, Exeter Street, Covent Garden."

And then she was gone.

I lay on my bed, immobile, my head pounding and my limbs aching. I did not stop shaking for a long time.

***

After that encounter, I seldom stayed home. I lodged with friends, in brothels, at my club.

I knew what the night-slayer had been telling me when she'd recited my name and house number. She meant that she knew who I was, where I lived, and where I went each day. She'd already known where I'd taken the child, where Lizzie lived. She must have followed me that night, had been following me ever since, skulking in the shadows, watching my every move. I'd heard stories of night-slayers stalking their victims for years, terrifying them, playing with them, making pets of them, all the while killing them slowly.

But months went by, and I did see not my night-slayer again. The months lengthened to a year. Her daughter grew and talked and ran. I could not stop going to visit her. She called me Uncle Robbie. My fears waned with time, and I fell into my old habits of drinking too much, lying too long abed, avoiding doing anything useful, visiting Lizzie when I could, and touching friends and Margery for money.

And I looked for the *drohner*.

I heard of a man in Wales who'd found one, and I made the journey. But it was not ours. Ours would have called to me, responded to the touch of my hand. This one did nothing. It was a dead black lump, drained of its might by decades in the dirt before the young Welshman had chanced across it while he'd been tending sheep and dug it up.

Every rumor, no matter how small, called me on heartbreaking treks across England, once to France, with only gin to comfort me, but to no avail. Someone had stolen our *drohner* and hidden it from us. One day, it would be as dead and drained as the one I'd seen in Wales, and the Archer family would fade to nothing.

One of the men I'd shown the thing to that fateful night was Daniel Almay, a lieutenant of my regiment, who shared my club and most of my life.

"Saw your sister-in-law last evening at Almack's," he said one night as he opened his box of snuff in the club's library and took a hearty pinch. "She looked a bit wan."

"She's ill," I said with some sadness. "She was increasing again this spring, but didn't come up to scratch."

"Good lord. I am sorry."

I shrugged, hiding my anger. When Margery had delivered her second stillborn child two months ago, Frederick had berated her. I'd gone to pay her a well-wishing visit and heard him lash out at her, calling her weak and a poor excuse for a woman.

I'd turned on Frederick and snarled that perhaps it was his seed that was wanting, not the receptacle. He'd struck me full in the face. I'd leapt at him, ready to do battle, but Margery had screamed at me, begging me to leave him alone.

I'd gone. A month had passed and then Margery had visited me in my rooms. She came in a hired hack, bundled in cloak and deep hood, without her maid or footman.

I watched her through bloodshot, aching eyes, a leftover of my night's oblivion of port and brandy and gin as she sat upright on a chair across the room, so very proper was Margery. She apologized for not inviting me to the house while she recovered, and then for Frederick's behavior toward me that day, but I waved it away.

"Don't worry," I said, my voice a rasp. "You needed time to heal, and old Freddy can't help being a right bastard."

Margery twisted her hands, pulling the soft leather gloves from her thin wrists. "Robert, I ... I so want to have a child."

"I know you do."

"I have been thinking on what you said." She studied the gloves, her lashes black against her pale face. "That perhaps it is not my fault that I have failed."

"No *perhaps* about it," I said, trying to sound cheerful. "It is not your fault at all. Do not let my brother wear you down. He is disappointed, and he looks for someone to blame."

She kept her gaze on her hands. "I know Frederick does not mean to be so beastly."

I disagreed. I was of the opinion that Frederick meant every word of his nasty declarations.

"I would do anything, I think, to have a

child." Margery finally raised her head and looked at me, and her cheeks went a dull shade of red.

A long moment of silence hung between us. Upstairs, a woman began shouting drunkenly. A male voice rose, coupled with heavy thumps on the floor. Flakes of loose gray paint floated down and rested on my sleeve.

"Margery ..."

She looked away, shamefaced. "I know it is in your best interest to keep me from conceiving."

She meant that if Frederick died childless, I inherited the lot. Land, wealth, the baronetcy, honor. A single child could cut me out of the succession forever.

I didn't give a damn.

"You are my sister-in-law," I said. "That means that as far as the law is concerned, you are my sister. With everything that goes with it." Anytime I had thought to comfort her in the way I'd learned such comfort from Lizzie, the forbidden nature of such a liaison had stopped me. Margery wasn't a bad sort, pretty in her own way, though tired and worn now. She'd been a beauty when Frederick had courted her—I had met her for the first time when I'd been on leave from trying to kill Frenchman on the Peninsula and had envied Freddie. He had everything, and a lovely woman on top of it.

"I know," Margery said, her voice nearly a whisper. "But you are Frederick's brother."

I stared into her unblinking brown eyes. I read shame there and beneath it, great hope. She trapped me with that pathetic hope.

So I lay with her, my brother's wife, piling sin atop sin. My gentleness surprised her, I guessed by the tensing of her muscles where she expected pain. I sensed her relax when she did not find it.

I went to Lizzie afterward and tried to erase the deed by committing more sin. My heart ached, and I had been ill at ease ever since.

Daniel Almay returned me to the present by saying: "I suppose she's feeling the loss of the *drohner*. You are not looking so fit yourself."

"May we speak on another subject?" I asked stiffly. I declined his offer of snuff, but I would kill for a gin. The club, alas, offered only the gentlemanly liquids of wine, brandy, and port.

"Not yet," Almay said. "I heard of someone else who recently surfaced with a *drohner*. Gregory Folkstone. He boasted it to me, like the bacon-brain he is."

"Folkstone?" I stifled a snort. "His grandfather was a butler."

"My point exactly. What is a butler's

family doing with a *drohner*? It either cannot be genuine, or belongs to someone else."

I sat back. "I don't believe him. If his family had owned it all this time, he would have told the tale before now. And if it is mine—stolen—why would whoever had stolen it suddenly hand it over to Folkstone?"

Almay held out his hands as he shrugged. "Who knows? But don't ignore this, Robert. I worry for you."

I sighed. "It would be stupid not to ask him. Do you know where he is tonight?"

Almay barked a laugh. "Unless he's at death's door, he'll be gaming. Losing all that beautiful blunt his grandfather built for posterity."

I thanked Almay for his information, joined him in a brandy, and left him.

Before I went in search of Folkstone, I paid a call on Derek Chase, the second gentleman I'd showed the *drohner* to before it disappeared.

The world regarded Derek as a silly fellow, but the world was wrong. He had a canny sense behind his affable smile that had built a fortune for him in the City. His simple tastes kept him in a pair of rooms off Jermyn Street where he lived in modest style. He greeted me at the door of those rooms with affection.

"Robert Archer, by all that's holy. Haven't seen you in an age. You look wretched."

He made me sit in his parlor while his manservant brought a bowl of brandy, water, and sugar.

"This is killing you, isn't it?" Derek asked, his eyes narrowing in concern. "Do not shake your head at me; you are fading, my dear fellow. I saw your brother the other day. White as a ghost and thin as a lathe. This is what comes from this wretched *drohner* business. Thank God my ancestors weren't titled and pedigreed and felt the need to have a *drohner*. The idea of putting all a dynasty's strength and hope into a hunk of stone is nonsense. If you lose it, you lose everything. You are vulnerable. Look at you."

"But with a *drohner*, we have the strength of giants," I answered, sincerely believing it. History had proved it—the Archers had been powerful until this disaster. "Someone out there wants to destroy our strength. And when I find that someone, he will answer for it."

I left him after another bowl of brandy to hunt Folkstone. As I popped in and out of every gaming hell in St. James's, a lightskirt attached herself to me. She wore a tight green silk that showed off her pretty ankles, and a large bonnet that hid her face.

"I'm out at pocket tonight, love," I told her. "And on a mad goose chase besides."

She followed me a little while longer, then drifted away. I never discovered Folkstone, but I found comfort in a cellar gin shop—a short way to hell at a penny a glass.

I dragged myself out at a time respectable people were just beginning to stir. The cold dawn light hurt my eyes, and I walked, half-blind, toward the river.

They waited for me at a turning near Charing Cross, two men armed with cudgels and death in their eyes. I fought madly, drawing blood with my knuckles, but they battered me soundly.

I saw my lightskirt out of the corner of my eye. She ran toward one of the thugs, lifted him from me, and slammed him to the pavement. The other stared in stunned surprise, and died with her fingers in his chest.

I rolled to my feet and ran. Or tried to. My legs shook and buckled, and I could not breathe. In considerable pain, I sagged against a wall and watched the night-slayer murder two men. She ripped out their throats and fed on their blood, while I slid to the ground in terror.

She came to me. She'd removed her bonnet from her sun-yellow hair, and her dark eyes held mine.

"Who were they?" she demanded. "Why did they try to kill you?"

"I do not know," I answered, trying to catch my breath.

"You do know." Her green silk was wet with blood, and blood had spilled from her mouth to dry in rivulets on her white throat. "You *know*. Think."

"I was looking high and low for Folkstone. Maybe someone does not want me to find him." I squeezed my eyes shut. "I told Derek." Had he betrayed me? Had he stolen the *drohner*, for whatever reason, and tried to stop me finding it? "Please, God, not Derek."

"Look at me," my night-slayer said.

I tried to turn away, drunk and weeping. She took my face in her strong hand and forced it to her. I gazed into her bloody face and the cold evil in her eyes, and quailed.

"You have not found your *drohner*, have you?" she asked. "You have not looked. You have killed yourself instead."

"What are you talking about?" I said wearily. "I've searched and searched. I've gone all over England—"

Her fingers dug into my jaw. "You have not looked hard enough. Else you would have found it. You have buried yourself because you fear the truth."

I was alone, aching, and sick. *What truth?* "Why are you trying to save me?"

"I told you why."

Because I'd saved her child. I was Androcles to her lion. I'd pulled the thorn from her paw when I'd taken the little girl to Lizzie. I wondered how long my parole would last.

"Your daughter is growing tall," I said. The girl had become dear to me, and the thought of her brought a faint smile to my cracked lips. "Her hair is the color of sunshine."

My night-slayer slid her hand to my aching chest, tracing a gentle curve over my ribs. "You have a good heart, Robert. I feel it, the goodness in you. It beats through your blood and your body. It is why you are dying."

"I don't . . . understand."

She smiled, cruel and animal-like. "Do you fear me?"

"God, yes."

"Good. Fear keeps you alive. Love and goodness will kill you." She leaned closer, her breath touching me. "Let me find the *drohner* for you."

I tried to shake my head "No..."

"I know where it lies, and why it lies there. You gave me a life. Let me give yours back to you."

I had no idea what she was talking about—how could she know? If the *drohner* were so easy to obtain, I'd have found it by now. "You saved me twice already," I pointed out. "Surely our bargain is finished."

The night-slayer gave me a pitying look. "Robert, you believe that the difference between life and death is breathing and not breathing. The battlefield taught you that. But the difference is so much more. I will give you that understanding, if nothing else."

My head ached and throbbed, and I knew I'd never stand up. "You give me riddles."

"Let me teach you the answers to them, then."

I roused my strength and shook off her hand. "No. You can't understand what this is all about. Our bargain is finished—you have no need to come to my aid again."

She dragged me to my feet with a power that terrified me. "Seek not to bargain with a night-slayer, Robert Archer. You will lose."

My night-slayer threw me aside with easy strength and walked away into the darkness.

After that night I remained stone-cold sober. I took little more than a glass of port or brandy every day and turned my face from gin shops. The haze receded from my world, and I saw with sharp outlines for the first time in years.

I saw that my brother was no more than an idiotic brute who enjoyed tormenting his wife because the law gave him leave to. I saw that I had succumbed to self-pity and self-indulgence not only over losing the *drohner*, but because I was poor, lonely, struggling, and resented the fact that Freddy had inherited everything. I had a long climb to make out of the abandon to which I'd sunk.

And I saw that my brother was dying.

I saw it in his thin hands, the weary look in his eyes, the pale outline of his lips. His walk had slowed, his steps had become clumsy, his hair thin and lank. A wasting disease, some whispered. The absence of the *drohner*'s protective magic, my friends said. The loss of honor, I knew inside myself. He'd never had much honor to begin with — the loss of the collective honor of the family had broken his heart.

I finally ran Folkstone to ground and flattered him into showing me his *drohner*. It was not ours.

He had it enshrined in his front parlor, in a japanned cabinet with a tiny lock. The polished black cube rested on a cushion of velvet, surrounded by junk — pressed flowers, a cork from the first bottle of port he'd drunk at Carleton House, a diamond stud given him by a lady.

Folkstone did not understand the *drohner* in the least. It was not some memento, to be shut in a curio cabinet until shown to any who asked. Folkstone beamed over his treasure, but I knew it for what it was, an imitation that some artist had made for him, probably for a ridiculous price. A pretty thing, but it did not have the depth, the resonance of old magics beating from the ancient past. I politely admired it, hiding my disgust.

A few months passed. I mulled over what my night-slayer had said, that I knew where our *drohner* was but feared to look for it there. My thoughts darkened and I did not like them. Easier to comb the city, keeping an ear open for any rumors or tales of a stray *drohner* where it did not belong.

My brother slowly sickened, and he would no longer receive me at the house. Margery was belly-full again. I assumed she'd had the intelligence to drag old Frederick off to bed the same night she'd lain with me so that he would not doubt the child was his.

Lizzie's brood grew to include a little boy with hair the same shade of brown as mine. Her good-natured lout of a husband either did not notice or did not care.

On one visit, I told Lizzie I loved her.

"Don't be daft," she whispered as we lay entwined on the blanket in the cellar. "I'm thirty-five if I'm a day."

I traced her cheek. "In all of the world, there is no woman with as good a heart as yours. Whatever happens to me, whatever happens to you—I love you as I love no other."

Lizzie flushed, pleased, and hid her face in my shoulder.

Of the other woman in my life, I saw no sign. I did not forget about her this time, and I had stopped drinking until she receded into the haze. I watched every shadow, every passage, every stray woman who passed me.

But I never saw the night-slayer ... until I went to Lizzie to pay what turned out to be my last visit.

Lizzie's husband was out, and I lingered a little longer than usual. When I put on my clothes and went out to Lizzie's front room, the little girl with sunshine hair came to me.

"Uncle Robbie," she said. "I have your bit of stone."

And she pulled out of her little apron the *drohner*, which had been missing for nearly three years.

I stared at it, dumbfounded. The tallow candlelight warmed its polished depths, and its underlying red streaks burned redder as I reached for it.

I felt its magics even before I touched it. I was an Archer, and generations of Archers great and ignoble had poured their magics and their hearts into it. They called to me across the years, and my fingers trembled as

I pressed the stone to my own heart.

The *drohner* was smooth to the touch, almost soapy-feeling. It had a heat of its own, which warmed my numb fingers. It sang to me, possessed me, welcomed me home. I closed my eyes, letting the peace of the thing spill over me.

"Robbie, are ye all right?"

I opened my eyes to find Lizzie at my elbow. She smelt of candle grease and lovemaking, and she watched me with tender concern.

"Where did you get it?" I asked the little girl.

"A lady brought it to me. She said you were looking for it."

I stared, alert. "What lady? Who was she?"

"She didn't give no name," the mite said. "She gave it to me and told me you needed it."

I looked at Lizzie in great alarm. "You did not let this woman into your house, did you?"

Lizzie watched me with eyes that held only curiosity. "No, we saw her in the market. She was polite spoken—a lady. Do you know who she was?"

A night-slayer. Whose daughter you've had the keeping of these last four years.

"I must go. I must ... " I trailed off, not certain what I had to do. I absently kissed

Lizzie on the cheek. "God bless you, Lizzie," I said and started away.

"Robbie."

Lizzie's voice sounded odd, and I turned back. She was twisting her plump hands in her apron. "Robbie, I think ye should not come back."

I stopped, stricken.

"Don't look at me like that. It's Jack, ye see."

Her husband. I made for her, anger rising. "What has he done? Has he hurt you? Does he know ... ?"

Lizzie's mouth softened into a fond smile. "He's not done a blessed thing. He don't say nothing, but ... He's getting on a bit, Jack is. And he ain't got no one but me."

I stared at her, hurt in my heart and the *drohner* singing in my soul. "You love the lout."

"That I do. I always have."

Yet, she'd spared some little corner of her heart for me. I went to her and touched her cheek. "He's lucky, is Jack."

Lizzie kissed my fingers. "I'll not forget ye, Robbie."

And I would never love another woman as strongly as I loved her. For all Lizzie eked out existence in the back streets of London with eight children and no money, she had more sense than the most sophisticated city trader, more courage than any regimental commander, more compassion, more caring than any gentlewoman I knew.

I kissed her lightly on the lips, my eyes wet. I slid the *drohner* into my pocket, tousled the little girl's sun-colored hair, and left Lizzie's house forever.

***

I sensed the night-slayer before I saw her this time. My sobriety had led me to a heightened state of awareness, so I was not startled when she fell into step beside me in the rainy March darkness as I made my way from Lizzie's street.

I did not ask her where she'd found the *drohner*. I thought I knew, and I feared the knowledge.

"If your brother dies," the night-slayer said in her clear, even voice. "You inherit the lot."

"His son does," I corrected her. "If Margery is carrying a boy and it lives."

"Likely you'd be appointed guardian, as his uncle. You'd have the care of Margery as well. She'd see you would not lose by it."

I stopped in the street. The fog-shrouded darkness was mostly empty—only one person pushed past us, grunting in irritation. "Why do you want Freddy to die?" I asked. "Why should *you* care what happens to me?"

The night-slayer stared at me with

fathomless eyes in the face of an ordinary, pretty young woman. "She is a beautiful child. You give your lover money for the keeping of her, don't you?"

"What I can spare, yes. Lizzie and her husband have nothing."

"And you have so little." The night-slayer cocked her head. "Why should you give it, for the child of a creature like me?"

I shrugged, though my chest was tight. "It seems the thing to do."

"You wish to keep her safe, so she will not end up prey for a night-slayer. So that one will not find her and make her like me. You want to give her a chance."

"Yes."

"And for that," she said simply. "I want everything for you." She paused. "What will you do with the *drohner*?"

I had it inside my coat, resting against my chest. "Return it where it belongs."

She studied me a moment, eyes glittering in the dim light. "I will go with you."

"No." Dear God, I did not want her in my brother's house, with Margery ... and my child.

She showed her teeth in a smile. "I will go anyway."

***

My brother's footman gave the night-slayer a disdainful look when we entered the house, clearly not understanding what she was. The night-slayer had dressed respectably enough this evening, but my brother leapt to the same conclusion his servant did.

Frederick entered the small sitting room and bathed us both in his sneer. "What are you doing here, Robert? With one of your doxies, no less?"

I took the *drohner* from my pocket and held it out to him.

Frederick's face drained of color, his mouth dropping open. "Dear God. How did you —"

"Take it."

I set it into his hands. Frederick stared at the *drohner* for one long moment, then he looked up at me, eyes burning in his white face. "You brought it back to me." He whispered. He looked at the black stone with deep reverence. "Do you feel it? It knows it's home. So long. It has been so long . . ."

"Reward him," my night-slayer said sternly to my brother.

Frederick looked up from the *drohner*, blinked. "What?"

"Reward him. For returning it."

Frederick's face regained color, and with it his old obstinacy. "Devil take him. He lost the bloody thing in the first place."

Frederick found himself against the wall

with the night-slayer's hand hard on his chest. She brought her face close to his and spoke in slow deliberation.

"You are an empty shell of a man," she said, her voice low and fierce. "Your brother, Robert, keeps his word to a filthy night-slayer who can smell his blood and could kill him in a flash. His honor runs deep within him. *You* believe honor lies in a piece of polished stone. You are a fool."

The night-slayer's fingers split the silk of Frederick's waistcoat and tore into the flesh below. Freddy screamed.

I ran across the room and flung myself on the night-slayer, but my grip could no more move her than I could have moved a stone monolith. "Let him go."

She turned to me, her eyes pools of night. "Without him, you can have everything. His house. His money. His wife. His *life*."

"I don't want them!" I shouted. "I don't want them."

The night-slayer's fingers eased back from Frederick, but only a fraction. "You have nothing. Keep the *drohner*. You can have his riches, his power."

"I don't want it if it makes me like him. The *drohner* is all he has."

The night-slayer regarded me a moment longer, then she wrenched her fingers from Frederick's chest. His blood covered her fingertips to the first joint, and Frederick moaned piteously.

"You are a singular man, Robert Archer," the night-slayer said. Her voice had quieted, her eyes suddenly looking almost human.

The door crashed open and Margery darted into the room. "What is happening? Frederick, what is the matter?"

"Get out," her husband gasped at her. "Robert has brought his tame night-slayer to kill us."

My night-slayer carefully sucked Frederick's blood from her forefinger. "I am not tame."

Margery did not appear to notice her. Her gaze fixed on the *drohner* that Frederick clutched in his shaking hands. "What is *that*?"

"The *drohner*," I said quietly. "I brought it back."

The color left Margery's face. She pressed one hand to her abdomen and the other to her mouth, then she turned and fled.

I went after her. For a small woman, Margery moved quickly. I did not catch up to her until she'd reached a bedchamber, where I found her vomiting into a basin.

"Margery," I asked in alarm. "What is wrong?" I touched her shaking back. "Is it the child?"

Margery did not answer. She lifted away

from the basin, her face wet with tears and spittle. She reached for a towel and hid her face in it.

"Not the child," my night-slayer said behind me. "It is guilt."

"Margery stole the *drohner*," I said, finally understanding.

I remembered now that she'd paid me a visit a few days before I realized the thing had gone from the box I'd locked it into. I never liked her coming to my meager digs, and I'd rushed out to a tavern around the corner to bring her decent food and drink. She could easily have broken the flimsy lock of the box in my desk and taken the *drohner*.

In my gin-riddled state I'd not bothered looking at the thing or noticing that its hum in my heart had gone until I'd had the hankering to see it again. My devastation at finding the box empty had been horrible. I'd frantically searched my rooms, thinking I'd moved it and hadn't remembered. I'd ended up on the floor in wretched despair when I realized it was truly gone, and had drowned my sorrows in still more gin.

"That she did," the night-slayer said.

Margery lowered the towel. She looked pinched and old as she turned to the night-slayer. "How did you find it?"

The night-slayer spoke matter-of-factly. "I followed you when you last went to look at it. I suppose you couldn't resist making sure it was still safe. You hid it in the crypt of the Archer ancestors. Clever. You would have 'found' it when you laid your dear husband to rest."

Margery's eyes filled with fury as wild as any night-slayer's. "Frederick is brutal. I hate him."

The night-slayer did not change expression. "Your husband will weaken and die without the *drohner*. Everything he is comes from it."

"I *want* him to die," Margery spat. "I want the child to be Robert's. I want—I want *him*."

I stared at Margery in shock and anger. "You sent men after me to kill me. How can you say you want me and then do that?"

Margery shook her head, her wisps of curls trembling. "To frighten you. To stop you looking for the *drohner*. I never meant them to harm you. You have been good to me."

In the silence, two droplets of water fell from her wet fingers and spattered on the floor.

"Even if Freddy dies, I can never marry you," I said slowly. "The law forbids a man marrying his brother's wife. Doesn't matter if the brother is dead."

Margery's face was flushed with anger, her eyes wet. "My husband lives. With the return of the *drohner*, he will go on living. He will grow strong again. I can't bear it."

I pried the towel from Margery, set it aside, and took her hands. "Margery, I will not let him hurt you. Trust me—he will not lay a finger on you."

Margery's tears spilled from her eyes, her lips trembling in stark fear. "You cannot prevent him. You are not always here—Frederick does not listen to you. He doesn't respect you."

I was more resolute, and certain, as I looked into my sister-in-law's eyes than I had ever been. "I will protect you, Margery. I shall tell old Freddy that if he ever harms you, I will send for my night-slayer and let her play with him."

The night-slayer turned from where she'd been pacing a restless circuit of the room. "I am not tame, as I told you," she said in a hard voice. "Even if I do come when you bid me, I may be too hungry, too desperate to let you stop me killing him and draining him."

I gave her a dour look. "That is the risk Freddy will have to take. When he raises his hand against Margery, he will remember you reaching in for his heart tonight."

Margery's brown eyes were red-rimmed, her face blotchy with her weeping and illness. She looked beaten down and defeated, but I still saw the pretty young woman, all ringlets and soft smiles, who'd been introduced to me in a ballroom by Freddy, proud of his catch, all those years ago. I swore I would make her beautiful again.

I do not think Margery believed me when I said I could keep my brother in check, but I would make Freddy believe it.

My night-slayer was right: Frederick thought honor lay in a bit of stone, so easily taken, so easily lost. The night-slayer, a beast of violence and blood, had far more honor in her than Frederick ever would. For love of a child, an innocent, my night-slayer had curbed herself; for hope of a child, quiet Margery had committed two crimes in the eyes of the world.

I quit the room and strode back through the passage that led to Frederick's sitting room. The night-slayer followed. "I will not always come when you call," she warned me, sounding displeased.

"Frederick does not have to know that," I said with grim humor. "It is likely, if I put the fear of God in him, that you will not have to bother with him at all."

Candlelight sparkled on the night-slayer's sun-colored hair. "Margery has bravery in her. She dealt her husband a mortal blow, stealing the *drohner*, and he could not do a thing about it. Margery did not like hurting you, I think, but she lived with that guilt to get to your brother. She will make him a formidable enemy."

I snorted. "Good. It is about time Margery had her own back. She will have him exactly where she wants him."

The night-slayer touched my hair. "And I have you." She released me and licked the last of Frederick's dried blood from her forefinger.

I gave her a startled look, but my night-slayer only smiled.

Androcles had never completely tamed his lion.

End

Author's Note

Thank you for reading! These three stories began life long ago and were then buried and forgotten as my publishing career went in another direction. I came across the stories again when I emptied my closets after a flood forced us to replace the flooring throughout the entire house.

This closet held a cardboard box of stories — about fifty in all — across several genres, mainly mystery and scifi/fantasy. Some had been sold to small magazines; others I'd never submitted.

I went through the stories and decided to publish the ones I liked best, rewriting and revising as needed. I had many of them saved to floppy disks (also in the box) — I had to purchase a three-and-a-half-inch disk drive I could plug in to my current laptop to retrieve the electronic copies.

The first story, *The Bishop's Lady*, features Émilie d'Armand, a young lady-in-waiting at the court of Louis XIV. I had written a complete novel about Émilie and about a third of another before I ran out of time to work on her stories. I also have a few incomplete short stories that I will at some point finish to be published, as well as the novels.

The second story, *A Soupçon of Poison*, features Kat Holloway, a cook, another sleuth I planned to launch in a series. I had written about a third of *Soupçon* before, again, I had to put this story aside.

I'm pleased to be able to revive the stories and present them here. As time permits, I hope to expand on these two lady sleuths.

For the last story, *A Matter of Honor*, I debated a long time before adding it to this collection. It is a historical mystery, with the flavor of the Captain Lacey Regency Mysteries, but of course, there is the vampire to consider. I decided to include the story here because it fit best with historical fiction. This is a standalone, with no other stories in this world, although I do like the alternate Regency I have created and might explore it further.

Thanks again for reading. I continue to write the Captain Lacey Regency mysteries (have plenty more stories to tell), but I'm also happy to revive my love of historical mysteries in general with this peek at sleuths and time periods that are of interest to me.

For more information on the Captain Lacey mystery series, and to stay informed about when I will publish more Émilie d'Armand and Kat Holloway stories, visit my website at

http://www.gardnermysteries.com.

While there, join my newsletter, or link to the newsletter directly at

http://eepurl.com/5n7rz.

I send out newsletters when I have a new release, or other important announcements about books and series.

Best wishes,

Ashley Gardner

Read on for an
Excerpt of

The Hanover Square Affair

Captain Lacey Regency Mysteries

Book 1

by Ashley Gardner

Chapter One

London, April 1816

Sharp as a whip-crack, a shot echoed through the mists in Hanover Square.

The mob in the square boiled apart, flinging sticks and pieces of brick as they fled the line of cavalrymen who'd entered the far side of the square. I hugged a rain-soaked wall as people poured past me, bumping and shoving in their panic as though I weren't six feet tall and plenty solid.

The square and the streets that led to it had been bottled with traffic all afternoon: carts, carriages, horses, wagons, and those on foot who'd been running errands or passing through, as well as street vendors crying their wares. The mob had stopped traffic in all directions, trapping inside the square those now desperate to get out. They scrambled to get away from the cavalry and their deadly guns, and bystanders scrambled to flee the mob.

I scraped my way along the wall, rough stone tearing my cheap gloves, going against the stream of bodies that tried to carry me along. Inside the square, in the eye of the storm, the cavalrymen waited, the blues and reds and canary yellows of their uniforms stark against the fog.

The man who stood in their gun sights had led the mob the better part of the afternoon: shouting, cursing, flinging stones and pieces of brick at the unfortunate house that was number 22, Hanover Square. Now he faced the cavalrymen, his back straight, his gray hair dark with rain.

I recognized the lieutenant in charge, Lord Arthur Gale of the Twenty-Fourth Light Dragoons. A few years before, on a Portuguese battlefield, I'd dragged young Gale out from under a dead horse and sent him on his way. That incident, however, had not formed any camaraderie between us. Gale was the son of a marquis and already a social success, and I, the only son of an impoverished gentleman, mattered little to the Gale family.

I did not trust Gale's judgment one whit. He had once led a charge so hard that he'd broken through a solid line of French infantry but then found himself and his men behind enemy lines and too winded to get back. Gale had been one of the few who'd returned from that charge, leaving most of the others, horses and men alike, dead.

"Gentlemen," the old man said to the cavalrymen. "I thank you for coming. We must have him out. He must pay for what he's done."

He pointed at the house—number 22, ground-floor windows smashed, front door's black paint gouged.

Gale sneered down at him. "Get along, man, or we'll take you to a magistrate."

"Not I, gentlemen. *He* should face justice. Take him from his house. Bring him out to me. I beg of you."

I studied the house in some surprise. Any man who could afford to own, or lease, a house in Hanover Square must be wealthy and powerful. I assumed he was some peer in the House of Lords, or at least a rich MP, who had proposed some unpopular bill or movement, inspiring a riot against him. The rising price of bread, as well as the horde of soldiers pouring back into England after Waterloo, had created a smoldering rage in those who suddenly found themselves with nothing. The anger flared every now and then into a riot. It was not difficult these days to turn a crowd into a violent mob in the space of an instant.

I had no idea who lived in number 22 or what were his political leanings. I had simply been trying to pass through Hanover Square on my way to Brook Street, deeper into Mayfair. But the elderly man's quiet despair and incongruous air of respectability drew me to him. I always, Louisa Brandon had once told me, had a soft spot for the desperate.

Gale's eyes were dark and hard. "If you do not move along, I will have to arrest you for breach of the King's peace."

"Breach of the King's peace?" the man shouted. "When a man sins against another, is that not a breach of the King's peace? Shall we let them take our daughters while we weep? Shall I let him sit in his fine house while mine is ruined with grief?"

Gale made a sharp gesture to the cavalryman next to him. The man obediently dismounted and strode toward the gray-haired rioter.

The older man watched him come with more astonishment than fear. "Is it justice that I pay for his sins?"

"I advise you to go home, sir," Gale repeated.

"No, I tell you, you must have him out! He must face you and confess what he's done."

His desperation reached me as white mists moved to swallow the scene. The blue and red of the cavalry uniforms, the black of the man's suit, the bays and browns of the horses began to dull against the smudge of white.

"What has he done?" I asked.

The man swung around. Strands of hair matted to his face, and thin lines of dried blood caked his skin as though he'd scratched himself in his fury. "You would listen to me? You would help me?"

"Get out of it, Captain," Gale said, his mouth a grim line.

I regretted speaking, unsure I wanted to engage myself in what might be a political affair, but the man's anger and despair seemed more than mob fury over the price of food. Gale would no doubt arrest him and drag him off to wait in a cold cell for the magistrate's pleasure. Perhaps one person should hear him speak.

"What has the man in number 22 done to you?" I repeated.

The old man took a step toward me, eyes burning. "He has sinned. He has stolen from me the most precious thing I own. He has killed me!"

I watched madness well up in his eyes. With a fierce cry, he turned and launched himself at the door of number 22.

End of Excerpt

About the Author

Award-winning Ashley Gardner is a pseudonym for *New York Times* bestselling author Jennifer Ashley. Under both names—and a third, Allyson James—Ashley has written more than 75 published novels and novellas in mystery and romance. Her books have won several RT BookReviews Reviewers Choice awards (including Best Historical Mystery for *The Sudbury School Murders*), and Romance Writers of America's RITA (given for the best romance novels and novellas of the year). Ashley's books have been translated into a dozen different languages and have earned starred reviews in *Booklist*. When she isn't writing, she indulges her love for history by researching and building miniature houses and furniture from many periods.

More about the Captain Lacey series can be found at www.gardnermysteries.com.

Or email Ashley Gardner at
gardnermysteries@cox.net

Made in the USA
Middletown, DE
05 June 2015